DATE DUE

3. 2016 5	

PRINTED IN U.S.A.

THE OKLAHOMBRES

Bill Doolin is a loving husband and devoted father, who had never killed another man. But he becomes a target for every U.S. Marshal in Oklahoma Territory when the people hail him as 'King of the Outlaws'. When Doolin and his gang, the Oklahombres, raise hell throughout the Twin Territories of Oklahoma and the Indian Nations, Marshal E.D. Nix sends three hundred of his best men out with orders to finish them. However, the Oklahombres are determined to be living legends — or die trying . . .

STEVE HAYES
AND BEN BRIDGES

◆

THE
OKLAHOMBRES

Complete and Unabridged

LINFORD
Leicester

First published in Great Britain in 2014

First Linford Edition
published 2015

A catalogue record for this book is available
from the British Library.

ISBN 978–1–4448–2609–8

Published by
F. A. Thorpe (Publishing)
Anstey, Leicestershire

Set by Words & Graphics Ltd.
Anstey, Leicestershire
Printed and bound in Great Britain by
T. J. International Ltd., Padstow, Cornwall

This book is printed on acid-free paper

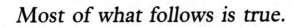

Most of what follows is true.

1

Kingfisher, Oklahoma Territory, March 14 1893

The boy — nine years old, with tangled hair the color of caramel taffy — burst through the church doors and started down the short aisle toward the people gathered around the altar. Before he could disrupt the proceedings, however, an undersized man lounging just inside the doorway reached out and snagged him by the arm.

'Whoa, there, boy!'

The youngster looked up at him. 'They . . . they're comin', Mr. Raidler!' he gasped.

Outwardly, William F. Raidler looked as placid as he always did. But the highly-educated Pennsylvanian, who was more familiarly known as 'Little Bill', fingered his trimmed chevron mustache with obvious concern. 'How close?' he asked.

'Three, four miles yet!'

Raidler handed the boy a silver dollar. 'Obliged,' he said. 'You get along, now.'

Delighted by the reward, the boy turned and ran for the exit. One of the doors had closed behind him but the other still stood ajar, and sunlight flared whitely from outside, for the spring day was bright.

Raidler hurried toward the altar. Three men in broadcloth suits that had seen better days were seated in the left front pew, listening attentively as the bald-headed preacher continued to conduct the marriage of William 'Bill' Doolin and Edith Marie Ellsworth without looking up from his *Book of Common Prayer*.

'Do you, William Doolin, take this — '

'I do,' said Doolin, turning his head a little as Raidler approached.

The preacher glanced up with as much of a scowl as he felt he could get away with. For a few seconds thereafter, the only sound was the urgent hiss Little Bill made whispering in Doolin's ear. At last Doolin nodded, looked at the three men seated in the front pew — Bill Dalton, Charley Pierce and Charles Daniel 'Dynamite Dick' Clifton — and his eyes flicked meaningfully toward the exit.

Wordlessly the three men rose, nodded to the preacher and then hurried for the doors, clapping their hats on as they went.

Doolin faced the altar again, a sober-faced, dark-haired man of average height and build, with a wide face and high cheekbones. His level eyes were a mild blue, his short, straight nose a path that led down to a generous mouth that was all but hidden beneath a thick handlebar mustache. He was thirty-five that year — which made him considerably older than his bride-to-be.

'You were sayin'?' he said.

The preacher finally collected himself. 'Do you, Edith Marie Ellsworth — '

'She does,' interrupted Doolin.

The preacher looked up at Edith.

'I do,' she nodded.

The preacher's mouth compressed. Marriage was a sacred institution, and it irked him to see it being trivialized by these people. But he knew better than to voice his disapproval. Though Bill Doolin had an enviable reputation for fairness, he wasn't a man to cross. Instead he just said: 'The ring?'

On Doolin's other side stood a tall man with pronounced cheekbones and a massive brush of a mustache, whose duties as Doolin's witness had required him to join Bill and Edith at the altar. His name was George Newcomb, but his friends mostly called him 'Bitter Creek'. Now Bitter Creek hurriedly fished the ring from a waistcoat pocket and handed it to Doolin. Doolin slipped it onto Edith's finger.

'Now join hands,' said the minister, 'and repeat after me — '

'Bill . . . ' hissed Raidler.

Doolin glanced at the preacher. 'Better get a shake on,' he advised.

Biting his tongue, the preacher rattled through the pledge with as much

4

dignity as he could before finishing with: 'In the name of the Father, and of the Son, and of the Holy Ghost — '

'Are they, uh, married yet?' asked Bitter Creek.

Taking a deep breath, the preacher said: 'I-now-pronounce-you-man-and-wife!' And then, testily: 'Yes. Happy now?'

Doolin and Edith shared a relieved smile and kissed. Though plain-faced, Edith had captured Bill's heart the minute they'd first met in Ingalls, a small, still-raw town about seventy-five miles north and west of Kingfisher. She'd occupied his thoughts in the eighteen months ever since, sometimes — as now — almost to the point of distraction.

Raidler sucked in an irritable breath because the kiss seemed to take forever. Bitter Creek must have thought the same thing, because he said: 'Bill, for God's sake ... ' Then, realizing he'd blasphemed, he glanced toward the rafters. 'Beg pardon, Lord. But we got to get *moving*, Bill!'

5

Bill reluctantly pulled away from his new bride. 'Meet you in Ingalls,' he told her, naming a town in which she often stayed with her friend, a hotel proprietress named Mary Pierce. 'Just as soon as I can.'

She nodded, her dark eyes suddenly glistening with the onset of tears. She was a little above five feet in height, and of slender build. Long auburn hair, now gathered in a bun at the back of her head, framed a pale, heart-shaped face. Her wedding dress was a simple pale gray, button-fronted affair with a round neck, worn with a white woolen shawl.

'I'll be there,' she promised.

'And you,' Bill said, handing the preacher some money, 'remember — this marriage never happened. Don't need no one knowin' about me an' Edith.'

The preacher nodded gravely.

Doolin, Bitter Creek and Raidler then ran for the exit. As they went, Little Bill dragged two handguns from under his coat and passed one each to his companions.

They burst out of the church into the warm March sunshine. Already mounted, Bill Dalton, Charley Pierce and Dynamite Dick were waiting in the front yard, Dick holding the reins to three other horses. Without breaking stride, Bill and the others stepped up to leather and prepared to ride.

They were just in time.

Down at the far end of Main Street somebody bawled: *'There they are!'*

Bill looked around and recognized the tall, funereal-looking deputy at the head of the posse now entering town from the south.

'Dammit! Time to make dust, boys!' he yelled, and gave heels to his gray horse.

*   *   *

As they galloped away from the church and rode hard for the north end of town, Deputy U.S. Marshal Bill Tilghman, in charge of the posse, sent his horse forging ahead of his companions.

Caught up in the moment, he drew his Peacemaker and thumbed off a shot. It missed Doolin, but warned him that Tilghman meant business.

The lawmen thundered past the church just as the preacher escorted Edith Ellsworth — Edith Doolin, as she now was — down the steps to a waiting buckboard. Edith had 'borrowed' the vehicle from her father, the postmaster of Lawson who was himself a part-time preacher.

Still clutching her small, already-wilting bouquet, she climbed onto the buckboard, striving to keep her emotions in check.

'I understand your need for . . . discretion,' the preacher said softly. 'But you cannot keep such a thing as a marriage a secret forever, Miss . . . Mrs. Doolin. Your parents — '

'I'll tell my parents upon my return home,' she replied. 'By then it'll be too late for them to do anything to stop it. But if anyone else were to learn of it — '

'I understand that,' said the preacher. 'But *you* must understand, even if you tell your parents *after* the event, it is still . . . '

His voice trailed away. He could see that her thoughts were elsewhere. In her mind Edith saw Bill and the others riding for their lives, the posse gradually, unstoppably closing on them. Shots would be traded, and though it would be difficult indeed to hit anything from the back of a charging horse, there was always the chance that one bullet among so many would find a target — perhaps even Bill himself —

Much as she didn't want to think about that, about becoming a widow within minutes of having become a wife, the possibility persisted, and made her throat tighten.

Then she looked down at the bouquet and remembered suddenly that today was not only her wedding day, but also her twentieth birthday. This was certainly not the way she had ever expected to start her married life.

But it was as the vows had said. For better, for worse, for richer, for poorer, in sickness and in health, to love, cherish and to obey . . . *till death us do part.*

With a slap of the reins the buckboard moved off, heading away from her husband, his friends . . . and the posse that was intent on capturing or killing them.

2

Fortunately, there was one further advantage that Bill and his self-styled 'Wild Bunch' had over their pursuers that Edith hadn't considered. Their horses were relatively fresh, having rested during the wedding ceremony; those of the posse had already been ridden hard and were in little mood to be ridden harder.

As Bill and his companions slowly but surely outdistanced the lawmen, he recognized a series of low, round hills to the north and east. Even though he cautioned himself to take nothing for granted, knowing that to do so was a sure route to a short life, he couldn't help surrendering to a sudden wild flare of exhilaration. Sweeping off his hat, he waved it madly above his head, and behind him, he heard one of boys yell, '*Yeee-hah!*'

Then they were all climbing a grassy slope, topping out in a bunch on its shaggy rim and descending the far side in a wild scramble with hardly a break in stride.

A mile later they spotted a stand of sawtooth oak. Within minutes the timber had swallowed them whole. Five minutes after that it thinned a little and they came to a stream, running shallow right now but deep enough to suit their purpose. Leading the way, Bill sent his gray mount, Possum, off the bank in a leap. The animal landed in an explosion of water. A tug on the reins turned Possum north, and the horse cantered downstream with the rest of the Wild Bunch following close behind.

A mile further on, the timber started thickening again — bald cypress mixed with a little hackberry and dogwood this time. Bill's gray climbed onto the far bank at a spot where a shelf of scattered shale and rock would leave few if any tracks.

They pushed deeper into the bosque,

now holding their mounts to a walk. At length Bill signaled a halt in a low-lying swale. Turning in the saddle, he caught Bitter Creek's eye. Bitter Creek nodded, and without having to be told, slipped a dented telescope from one saddlebag and rode back through the trees in order to glass their back-trail.

Bill and the others sat their horses in the muddy clearing, waiting. Bit chains jingled, horses stamped and blew. Bill reached forward and ran a hand along Possum's neck.

Finally Bill Dalton growled: 'That was too damn' close. I mean, I *told* you you was takin' a fool's chance, decidin' to get wed in Kingfisher.'

'We got clear, didn't we?' Bill replied.

'Just about. But it could just as easy've gone the other way.'

'Well, it didn't. So let that be an end to it.'

A short time later Newcomb rode back in.

'See anyone?' asked Bill.

'That country's just about as empty

as Satan's heart,' Bitter Creek replied. 'Wouldn't surprise me if them fellers haven't turned tail an' gone back the way they come.'

'That was Tilghman on our trail,' Dynamite Dick reminded them. 'Tilghman *never* quits.'

'Tilghman's just another fool with a badge,' said Dalton. He was a short, humorless man of twenty-seven, with a square face and strangely lusterless blue eyes. 'I don't know why you fellers rate him so high.'

Raidler expected Bill to respond to that, for Bill had little time for Dalton but great respect for the deputy. When he didn't, the little Pennsylvanian studied him closer and saw to his surprise that Bill, so fired-up just a short time before, now sat near-lifeless in his saddle.

'What is it, Bill?' he asked quietly.

Bill eyed him briefly. 'Nothin'.'

'Doesn't look like that from where I'm sitting. What's wrong?'

Though Bill was reluctant to confess

14

to any kind of weakness in front of Dalton, he was suddenly compelled to unburden himself. 'I don't know . . . just . . . sometimes it seems like I'm always headed in the wrong direction. You fellers ever get like that?'

Though no one replied, the question had a sobering effect on them all. They swapped glances, each one seeing the truth of the statement in the expressions of his companions; that while there were tremendous highs in the way they'd chosen to live, there could also be some God-awful lows.

One by one it dawned on them that not more than thirty minutes ago Bill had been getting married. Now here he was — here *all* of them were — fighting to stay one step ahead of a posse all over again.

'Damn,' muttered Dynamite Dick.

He spoke for them all.

'Come on, fellers,' Bill muttered glumly. 'Let's ride.'

* * *

15

On the long, cautious trek east to the hideout not far from the town of Beaver Creek, Bill's thoughts were dominated by Edith. He felt guilty that this of all days should have worked out as it had. He thought of Edith now, returning to Lawson, where she would tell her folks what she had done — what *he*, Bill, had talked her into doing. There'd be shock, disappointment, tears and maybe some yelling from Edith's old man. But her folks were good people at heart. They'd get all that out of their systems and then they'd decide they had no choice but to make the best of the situation. Edith would be all right.

Still . . .

This had been her wedding day. Her *birthday*, dammit! She'd deserved so much more, and if he'd been half the man he thought he was, he'd have given it to her. But he was too far along the trail to change his ways now . . . wasn't he?

He'd been born in Johnson County, northwestern Arkansas, in 1858. When his father died seven years later, Bill had promptly pitched in to help run the small family farm along Big Piney Creek. But eventually he'd grown tired of farming and left home for pastures new.

He was twenty-three when he signed on with a freight train headed for Indian Territory, as Oklahoma was then known, but it was in Caldwell, Kansas, that he had the good fortune to meet a rancher named Oscar D. Halsell.

The two men had hit it off at once, and Halsell had pretty much hired him on the spot. Oscar had eventually taught him to read and write, too, so's he could help out with the ranch bookwork.

But the killer winter of '82-'83, followed by a government order for ranches to remove their stock from the so-called 'Unassigned Lands' prior to settlement in 1889, had pretty much ruined Oscar Halsell. And without his steadying influence, Bill started to feel restless and edgy. Friends like Tulsa

Jack Blake, Charley Pierce and the Dalton boys, Grat, Bob and Emmett, all felt the same way.

With little or no work to be had, it seemed only *natural*, somehow, for men in their position to take up the owlhoot — and that's what they did.

It was funny, the way things panned out sometimes, Bill thought suddenly. The Dalton boys had eventually met their match in Coffeyville, Kansas, when a double bank robbery went disastrously wrong, Grat and Bob had been killed and Emmett was sentenced to life imprisonment.

A wiser man would have taken that as an omen and quit the larcenous life altogether. Instead, Bill had decided to form his own gang, his Wild Bunch. Now it was the youngest of the Dalton boys, also called Bill, who rode with them.

Not that thinking of Bill Dalton was calculated to lighten his mood any. He turned now, threw a seemingly casual glance over one shoulder at the Dalton brother and saw him staring holes into Bill's spine.

Talk was that Dalton had once been a respectable businessman and had even served in the California legislature, but for all that he'd envied his wilder and more famous brothers. He'd also made the mistake of believing all the hogwash they'd written in the papers after Coffeyville, about how he'd been consumed with a need to avenge them. That kind of reckless journalism had planted a dangerous seed in young Dalton, for he'd quickly grown obsessed with becoming even more notorious than the rest of his clan put together.

So he'd come to the Oklahoma Territory to make a name for himself, and that's where his trail had crossed with Bill's.

There was just one problem.

Dalton didn't seem to understand that there could only ever be one leader of any gang. Decisions had to be made by one man and one man alone, not by committee. The leader had to weigh the course of each action he took, make sure it was in the best interests of the gang as a whole, and then enforce it, if needs be.

But Dalton didn't see it that way. He never stopped challenging Bill for the right to lead the gang, and though he never came right out and said what was on his mind, he'd throw out veiled — and sometimes not-so-veiled — comments that were meant to undermine him in the eyes of the others.

Bill's mood darkened.

The time was coming when such sniping would no longer be enough to satisfy Dalton's need to be top hand. Sooner rather than later there'd be a showdown between them, and then it would be winner take all.

It wasn't a prospect that Bill looked forward to. In fact, right now the life of the outlaw was starting to pall on him. It might look romantic to those who held down steady jobs and never had to sleep with one eye open. But the truth was very different. It was a miserable existence, most times . . . and yet, God help him, he was as addicted to it as other men were addicted to booze, to women or to morphine.

Behind him he heard Dalton grumbling about something or other. *Dalton.* That man was worse than a burr in his boot.

All right, he told himself. He needed to make things up to Edith and square himself away with her folks, and to do that he needed money. He also needed to reassert his authority over the rest of the boys before Dalton could talk them into mutiny.

The answer to both problems was a new job. And perhaps the introduction of a little new blood into the gang — men whose loyalty to him was without question — and a new name to go with it.

He couldn't say why, but he kind of liked the sound of . . . *The Oklahombres.*

3

The westbound Baldwin 4-4-0 was building to its top speed of seventy miles an hour when the headlamp picked out a crude sign ahead that warned DANGER — BRIDGE OUT!

The engineer scowled. Cimarron, Kansas, lay barely half a mile behind them. Why hadn't someone thought to let him know about the bridge back there, before he'd pulled out, bound for Santa Fe?

He quickly grabbed the brake handle and hauled it back as far as it would go. The spinning wheels clamped tight, slipped a little until they found traction again, and then started throwing up sparks. For long seconds steel clawed against steel with a banshee wail.

The Southern California and New Mexico Express slewed on for another ten yards, then finally screeched to a halt.

The engineer and his fireman both

sagged. Up ahead, the bridge was just visible in the beam of the headlamp. They'd averted disaster by a matter of yards.

But when the engineer and the firemen looked a little closer, they saw that the bridge wasn't out at all.

In which case —

Before they could reach the obvious conclusion, four riders came up out of a rock-strewn gulley that ran roughly parallel to the tracks, three of them with guns in hand, the fourth balancing a sledgehammer across his lap. The faces of the newcomers were hidden by flour-sack hoods.

'Aw, shoot,' muttered the engineer, and spat.

Drawing rein alongside the cab, Bill thumbed back the hammer of his Colt and said: 'You, engineer. Get on down here.'

The engineer was a sturdy-looking fifty-year-old with a wrinkled, saddle-leather face beneath a coal-smudged cap. He stared back at Bill for a moment, then did as he was told, muttering darkly about the schedule he was expected to keep, and how this here robbery was going to throw it right out.

It was a little after one in the morning of June 11, and the only other source of light in the vicinity was a scattering of stars and a thin sickle moon.

When the engineer dropped heavily to the right-of-way, Bob Dalton, sitting his horse alongside Bill, threw down the sledgehammer, then drew his own handgun. The sledge landed hard in the crunchy ballast at the engineer's feet. The engineer looked at it for a moment, then said: 'What the hell you want me to do with this?'

'The Wells Fargo car,' said Bill. 'Move.'

The engineer picked up the sledge and trudged back along the train with the robbers walking their horses along behind him. Silhouettes appeared at the carriage windows, then hastily withdrew as the two remaining robbers — former

Kansas cowboy 'Tulsa Jack' Blake and Dynamite Dick Clifton — waved their handguns threateningly.

Painted the same dull red as dried blood, the Wells Fargo car was a long, sturdy carriage built out of hard wood and strap-steel. It was largely featureless except for the small, barred windows set high in the walls and a little stub of stovepipe projecting from its slanting roof.

'Henry Harper!' yelled the engineer, thumping against the padlocked sliding door. 'It's me out here, Eddie Applegate! Don't you get no ideas about usin' that there shotgun o' yourn, Henry, 'cause you'll more'n likely kill me with the first blast, an' neither of us wants *that* to happen!'

There came no immediate reply. Then a voice called warily: 'What's happenin' out there, Eddie?'

The engineer threw a glance at the hooded men crowded behind him. 'We're bein' robbed,' he said wearily. 'Now, you just set easy, Henry. No call for anyone to get hurt . . . uh, right, you boys?'

'Right,' said Bill.

'Now, these fellers know you can't open up for 'em, even if you was so-minded. That's why I got to smash this here padlock an' let 'em in, right? So just you set tight, Henry, and when I get the padlock off, you let 'em have what they want and we all go away happy.'

Dalton gestured impatiently with his gun. 'Get on with it.'

The engineer raised the sledgehammer above his head and brought it down with ringing force on the padlock. The padlock jumped and dented a fraction, but continued to hold firm.

'Again,' said Dalton.

As the engineer did as he was told, Bill divided his attention between the Wells Fargo car and the few twinkling lights that marked Cimarron, away to the east. Even at this late hour, it was only a matter of time before someone back there noticed the stalled train and wondered why it had stopped. He

26

wanted to be long gone before whoever it was got curious enough to come and find out.

Still, he'd figured the risk was worth it. He'd learned that the express was carrying ten thousand dollars through to Santa Fe. That kind of money, even split four ways, would buy a whole lot of making-up to Edith. And such a haul could only strengthen his position as leader of the Oklahombres, as he'd now come to think of the gang.

It had been a busy few weeks, and though he'd only brought three other men on this job, he'd recruited several new members, including Tulsa Jack and Little Dick West.

Dalton, of course, had been quick to realize that Bill was deliberately enlisting men who'd back him against any attempt he, Dalton, might make to take over the gang. That's why he'd brought in one of his own cronies, a surly-tempered man in his early forties by the name of George 'Red Buck' Weightman.

Bill had taken an instant dislike to Weightman, and not just because he was a known killer and horse-thief. One look into Weightman's heavy-lidded eyes told him that he'd never be able to trust the man in a tight spot. Still, he didn't want to antagonize Dalton any more than he had to, so he'd told Weightman to come ahead and welcome.

Encouraged by that, Dalton had continued to seize every opportunity he could to call the shots — like right now, for example.

'Come on, damn you!' he cursed.

The engineer turned to face him. He was breathing hard and his face shone with sweat. 'Damn' thing . . . won't . . . budge,' he gasped.

Dalton leveled his Colt at the man. 'Then *make* it budge,' he hissed.

Bill quickly knocked Dalton's gun-arm down. 'Dick,' he called.

Dynamite Dick immediately kneed his horse forward. He'd blown three fingers off his right hand whilst playing with explosives in his youth, but that hadn't taught him any kind of lesson. He'd still gone on to become a robber, safe-cracker and rustler of long experience. Now the handsome, clean-shaven outlaw dismounted, rummaged in one saddlebag and brought out a long, yellow-wrapped stick of ready-capped nitroglycerin, from which hung a foot-long length of Bickford Safety Fuse.

'Better move back, boys,' he advised. 'You too, Applecrate, or whatever your damn' name is.'

As they did so, Dick produced a strip of rawhide and tied the nitro to the cold iron handle on the express car door. When he was finished, he struck a match and held the flame to the tip of the fuse. When the fuse started sparking, Dick followed his own advice and quickly dragged his horse back down into the gulley, where he joined the others.

Ten seconds later the charge went off.

The side of the car disappeared in a burst of flame, and the ground rocked underfoot. Splintered wood was hurled back into the car. When the smoke thinned, a few small flames could be seen licking at the ragged hole where the door had been.

The Oklahombres came back up out of the gulley, the engineer, Applegate, following behind them. Bill and Dalton pushed ahead, knowing they *really* had to work fast now. They swung down, passed their reins to the man nearest them — Tulsa Jack — then climbed into the car.

The car was a mess, with charred, splintered wood everywhere. A roll-top desk had been flung onto its side, spilling paperwork and half-sorted mail across the floor. The express messenger, Henry Harper, lay directly opposite the shattered doorway, hands pressed to his ears and a ruined Greener shotgun close by. He was in his early forties, balding prematurely, but with a thick red beard.

Ignoring him, Bill and Dalton looked around, saw two cast-iron safes sitting up against the right-side wall and hurried over to inspect them. One was smaller than the other, and bolted to the floor. The larger, free-standing one — presumably the one that was being transported to Santa Fe with ten thousand dollars inside it — had something Bill had only previously read about, and he swore.

'What is it?' growled Dalton.

'Timer lock,' Bill replied, gesturing. 'They fit 'em that way so's they can't be opened till they reach where they're goin'.'

'Can't we blow it?'

'We don't have the time.'

'Then we'll have to take it with us.'

'It's too damn' heavy for that.'

'Then what the hell do we *do?* You promised us ten grand, Bill!'

Bill stood up, turned to the express messenger. 'You,' he said.

The blast had rendered Harper temporarily deaf, and he gave no indication of having heard. Bill went over, tapped him on the shoulder, and the man started. Bill jabbed his Colt at the safes.

'How can we force that timer lock?' he asked.

Harper shook his head and pointed to his ringing ears. There were tears in his eyes and he looked like hell. Pointing to the larger safe, Bill mimed turning the handle and opening the door.

Harper shook his head and, unaware that he was doing it, shouted: 'You can't open it. No one can, till it reaches Santa Fe.'

Briefly Bill's shoulders dropped. But ever the optimist, he told himself that maybe he'd called it wrong: maybe the big money was in the smaller safe instead. He jabbed his Colt at it. 'Open it,' he said, and made the same crude mime.

Slowly Henry Harper crawled across the floor. Dalton booted him in the backside to speed him up. Clumsily, for his head was still spinning, Harper used one shaking hand to work the dial on the smaller safe. After a moment or so he worked the ornate brass lever and the door opened. Dalton shoved him aside and looked inside.

'What've you got?' asked Bill, thinking: *Ten grand. Say it's the ten grand we came for.*

Dalton said bitterly: 'Hardly enough to make it worthwhile, that's what!'

He turned with his hands full of envelopes and packages, and Bill slipped his gun away and pulled a gunnysack from the pocket of his jacket. As Harper clawed his way back to his feet, Dalton quickly transferred the contents of the safe to the sack.

'All right,' Bill said when the safe had been cleaned out. 'Let's move it!'

But as they turned for the door, Harper, the world still reeling around him, suddenly stumbled toward Dalton. Dalton saw the movement from the corner of one eye, twisted around and shoved the express messenger away from him.

For two long seconds, as his temper built and kept on building, he stared Harper right in the face. He was keyed-up — they all were — but more than that he was furious with the pitiful size of the night's take.

And that's why he shot Harper point-blank in the stomach.

The bullet folded Harper in two and threw him back against the opposite wall. He hit with a thud, then collapsed into a hunched-up sitting posture, dead.

For a moment everyone save Dalton was shocked to immobility by what had happened. Then Bill spat: *'You sonofa-bitch!'*

Dalton wheeled around to face him, his Colt still up, its barrel pointed toward Bill's belly, anger now clear in his usually lifeless eyes. Again time seemed to stand still as each man stared at the other. Then Bill brought the gunnysack around, batted Dalton's gun aside and with his other hand slapped him, hard.

Dalton rocked sideways.

'Give me one good reason why I

shouldn't gun you down right here an' now,' Bill snarled.

'Try it,' Dalton invited. 'See where it gets you.'

For a moment then it looked as if Bill would do just that, until Tulsa Jack's voice broke the impasse.

'We got company, Bill! Delegation from Cimarron, looks like!'

Bill's mouth clamped tight. 'All right,' he said. 'Let's get out of here!'

As he hopped down to the right-of-way, he reached into his jacket pocket and withdrew a handful of bills in various denominations. These he shoved toward the pale-faced Applegate. 'See that your friend in there gets buried good,' he said. 'And you,' he added, glaring at Dalton. 'You ever shoot another unarmed man in my company, Bill, I'll *kill* you.'

A heavy, ominous silence settled over them.

A second later gunfire split the night as the delegation from Cimarron galloped out of the darkness.

4

As they rode south, away from the stalled train and the anything-but-welcoming committee from Cimarron, Bill fought hard to keep his temper in check. The shooting of the express messenger had left a sour taste in his mouth. He didn't go for killing unless it was necessary, never had. But so help him, he was starting to think more and more that it might be necessary for Dalton.

The posse ended up dogging them for about three miles, often letting off wild shots just to let them know they were still around. After a time they quit and the night fell quiet but for the pound of hooves, the jingle of harness and the heavy breathing of hard-riding men. Finally Dalton pushed his mount out ahead of his companions and then tugged his horse around so that they had no choice but to draw rein sharply.

'You got a problem?' Bill asked, holding Possum in check.

'No problem,' Dalton replied. 'But I reckon we should divvy up.'

'Are you loco? With a damn' posse on our heels?'

'They've given up,' said Dalton.

'You willin' to take a chance on that?'

'Uh-huh.'

Bill glanced at the others. 'What about you fellers?'

Tulsa Jack and Dynamite Dick shrugged uncomfortably, not really wanting to take sides. 'I reckon we're safe enough now,' said Dick.

'So let's divvy up,' Dalton said again. 'See just how much tonight's little, ah . . . *enterprise* . . . earned us.'

Bill dismounted, left Possum ground-hitched, then emptied the gunnysack onto the ground. He knew what Dalton was up to. The sonofabitch wanted to humiliate him, discredit him any way he could in the eyes of the others.

By moon- and starlight he carefully

added up the night's take. It was close to a thousand dollars.

'But not the ten thousand you promised us,' said Dalton.

Bill looked up at him. 'No guarantees in this line of work, Bill,' he replied, his tone hard.

'The hell you say!' Dalton snorted. 'We risk our lives for — '

'There was precious little risk involved, the way it was planned,' said Bill. 'And each of you'll take away two hundred and fifty dollars for not much more'n twenty minutes' work. You don't like it, Bill, you ride on.'

'You don't get rid of me that easy.'

'Too bad. You're beginnin' to vex me considerable.'

Before Dalton could reply, Bill divvied up as fast as he could and gave each man his share. 'Now, let's ride,' he said when he was finished. 'We still got a far piece to cover before we're back on home ground.'

★   ★   ★

Dawn found them forty miles from Cimarron and about the same distance again from the Oklahoma border. By then men and horses both were in sore need of rest. Safe haven was provided by a remote canyon Bill knew, and in which they ended up spending that entire day.

They pushed on early the following morning. The town of Meade lay somewhere up ahead, and to avoid it they swung northeast. Late afternoon they came to a ranch where they were greeted — warily — by a tall, lean man of about forty, with shaggy black hair and a mostly toothless mouth. He came out into his yard the minute they appeared on the horizon, and stood watching until they'd walked their mounts in. Finally he shoved his black felt hat to the back of his head, looked Bill straight in the face and said: 'You'd be Doolin, I reckon.'

Try as he might, Bill couldn't completely mask his surprise. 'Would I, now?' he hedged.

'Had a feelin' you'd show up sooner or later.'

'Why'd you say a thing like that, mister?'

'Had Frank Healy out this way not two hours ago, lookin' fer you.'

Behind Bill, the others exchanged looks. Frank Healy was the sheriff of Beaver Creek. 'He's a little out of his bailiwick, ain't he?' asked Dalton, uneasily. 'Beaver County's across the line, an' we're still in Kansas.'

'The line's only two, three miles south, so he ain't too far off his patch,' the rancher pointed out. 'He said you fellers robbed a train up north.'

'And how might he've heard that?'

'Telegraph,' said the rancher. 'Frank says they've already put out a reward on you fellers.'

'Did he, now?' asked Dalton, hand moving toward his pistol.

'Oh, you got nothin' to fear from me,' the rancher added hurriedly. 'I don't get involved in another man's business, never have, an' my kin is jus' the same. You're welcome here, boys. All I ask if that you leave us as you found us.'

'We can do that,' said Bill.

'Then it looks like you an' me can do business,' said the rancher. He wiped his palm on his pants and then offered his hand. 'Name's Tainter,' he said as they shook.

'What else did you hear, Mr. Tainter?'

'That's about it.'

'What about this here reward?' asked Tulsa Jack.

'Well, as I understand it, it was a thousand dollars a head to begin with.'

'To *begin* with?'

'Ayuh,' said Tainter. 'Then Wells Fargo chipped in four thousand, an' the good State o' Kansas added another two.'

'And that's for *each* of us?'

Tainter nodded.

Bill and the others traded glances. On the one hand, there was a perverse kind of pride in their newfound notoriety. On the other, they knew that such a reward would eventually make them men hunted past all reason.

'You fellers look like you c'd use some coffee an' cake,' said Tainter.

'We could, at that.'

'Then light a while. Figure Frank an' his posse'll be long gone by this time.'

Tainter proved to be a good host. They ate well, extended the courtesy he requested to his family, and in the big barn rested both themselves and their mounts. The afternoon passed slowly and Bill luxuriated in the peace, for he didn't get too much of it in his line. Just before dusk, however, he rose and told the others to ready their mounts for the final push into Oklahoma. Reluctantly, they did so.

Within twenty minutes the Tainter place had fallen behind them.

'I swear, I'm gettin' too old fer this life,' said Dynamite Dick about a mile later. 'I reckon I could'a been happy, livin' peaceable back there with them folks.'

Around them, the sun was setting slowly across downward-sloping fields of buffalo grass bordered by stands of cottonwood. As near as Bill could tell, the Fort Supply Military Reservation was maybe ten miles north and east — another landmark to avoid.

Tulsa Jack snorted. 'How the hell old are you, anyway, Dick? Twenty-five or thereabouts?'

'Thereabouts.'

'Huhn. You're still just a kid. I got about ten years on you, an' you don't hear *me* complainin'.'

'That's 'cause you've been ridin' the owlhoot since Hector was a pup. Had more time to get used to it.'

'Well, you got that right. I'm a bad man of long standin'. Compared to me, you're just a be — '

Before he could finish there came a distant popping sound. A moment later a meaty hole punched into the side of Jack's horse and with a high scream it crashed onto its side, spilling the man himself into the tall grass.

'Dammit!' yelled Dalton, twisting around. 'It's Healy's posse!'

5

Bill yelled: *'Dick!'*

Dick needed no further instruction. As Bill tore his Winchester from its scabbard, Dick kneed his horse up alongside the fallen Tulsa Jack and thrust down one arm. Though winded by the fall, Jack had managed to roll free of his dying horse and now lumbered back to his feet. He grabbed Dick's wrist and swung himself up behind the other man, and then Dick gave his mount a jab of the heels and it tore away toward the south.

Bill levered a shell into the breech and slammed the Winchester to his shoulder. *'Let's buy 'em some time!'* he called to Dalton.

But there was no response.

He chanced a quick look around and swore. Dalton was already making good speed toward a cluster of rocks about half a mile distant.

'Sonofabitch!'

Furious, Bill turned his fidgety gray back toward the knot of horsemen now galloping over the eastern horizon. There was an even dozen of them, and for all his faults Dalton had been right — it *was* Frank Healy and his posse.

Another firecracker rattle of gunfire punched through the sunset. Teeth clenched fit to shatter, Bill fired, levered and fired again, setting up a fusillade of his own to slow the newcomers.

It worked, after a fashion. The knot of riders broke ranks as they fought to control their nervy horses, and began to spread out. But still they came on, just a little warier is all. Bill sent another flurry of shots at them, and that made them stop, a few dismounting to seek cover behind their mounts and reaching for their own long guns as they did so.

Bill threw another look toward the south. Dalton was already just a dot in the powdery distance, Dick and Tulsa Jack following in the same direction,

45

Dick's horse carrying the double weight gamely but with obvious effort.

Then the posse started returning fire and Bill told himself it was time to get the hell out of there. He put a quick mercy bullet into Jack's squealing horse, then shoved the Winchester away and hauled Possum around all in one motion, and the gray launched into a gallop.

Another flurry of gunshots chased him, but he figured the range was too long and the light too poor for them to stand any chance of hitting him.

He was wrong.

Even as he thought it, something drilled him in the left heel and knocked his leg forward even as he himself tilted backwards. He swayed dangerously as Possum, equally startled, broke stride. Then the horse righted and continued carrying him on, but the damage was already done, and Bill was no longer in position to do anything but clutch his reins and hang on for dear life.

The pain in his leg wrenched at him.

He screwed his eyes shut and clamped his teeth against it. *I been shot*, he thought. *Dammit, I been shot!*

Dimly he heard another volley from behind him, but there were no further hits. His ruined boot seemed to fill with liquid, and every jolting pace Possum took sent a wave of agony through him. He leaned forward over the horse's neck and puked. His eyes opened, he saw the ground flashing along beneath him and was shocked at how quickly the sun was setting.

More gunfire jolted him out of the daze into which he had unknowingly fallen. He sat straighter in the saddle, saw that his companions had made it to the jumble of rocks, dismounted and were taking up positions within them to give him covering fire.

As he thundered toward the spill of boulders, Dick and Jack loosed off a series of shots that sent their pursuers scattering again. Hit in the chest, one horse went down forehooves first, somersaulted and landed on its rider, killing him instantly. Another posse man yelped, dropped his Colt, grabbed his shoulder and slumped in the saddle.

Bill rode on, looked up as the rocks came closer, saw Dalton to the right and a little above Jack and Dick, his own saddle gun shoved against his shoulder, one lusterless eye squinted down as he took aim —

Taking aim at me, Bill thought.

It became clear to him then, even through the wracking pain, just how Dalton was going to take over the gang — *by killing the man who was already leading it.*

Again time stood still, and it seemed for an instant as if Bill and Dalton were the only two people left in the whole wide world. He felt that their eyes met, though he knew that motion and distance made that almost impossible. Then Dalton tilted the barrel of his Winchester a tad and started adding his fire to that of his companions. Another posse-man twitched, blood spraying from a thigh wound.

He spared me, Bill thought. *But not from any sense of mercy.*

No: Dalton had probably realized he'd have a hell of a time explaining how Bill had come to be shot from the front while the posse was behind him. And hell, Bill was already leaking so much blood that for all Dalton knew, murder might not even be necessary.

Then he was in the cover of the rocks and bringing Possum to a clumsy, slithering halt. He would have fallen from the saddle, but all at once Dick was there to help him dismount. Vaguely he was aware that the gunfire had turned sporadic and was gradually petering out altogether.

'What . . . what's happenin' back there?' he managed as Dick sat him down as gently as he could.

'They're makin' dust!' Tulsa Jack called down over one shoulder. 'Guess they'd sooner dish it out than take it!'

'They'll be back,' growled Dalton, coming down off the rocks with his rifle held slantwise across his chest. 'You sing out if they show 'emselves again, Jack!'

'Yo!'

Coming down onto level ground, Dalton said: 'We better keep movin'.'

'Don't talk foolish,' said Dick. 'Look here, Bill's been hit.'

Dalton looked at Bill's bloody foot. 'Then we'll have to leave him behind,' he decided. 'He'll slow the rest of us down, we try to take him with us.'

Bill looked up at him, his smile cold and unpleasant as the pain subsided to a dull roar. 'Like you . . . left the rest of us behind when that posse first . . . showed up?' he asked.

Dalton bristled. 'You told us to ride!'

'I told Dick to help . . . Jack, there. I figured you an' me, we'd . . . make a stand and buy 'em some time to get clear, what with Dick's horse . . . carryin' double. Next thing I knew, I was all by my . . . lonesome.'

'You better not be callin' me a coward — !'

'I don't . . . have to,' grunted Bill. 'A

50

man's actions generally . . . speak for 'im.'

'Why, you — '

'Quit your argufyin',' snapped Dick. He quickly inspected Bill's foot, then took out a knife and cut the boot off. It was all Bill could do not to howl at the pain of it. At last Dick inspected the wound by the last of the day's light.

'Hell,' he said.

'That bad?' asked Bill.

'Busted up some,' said Dick. 'Figure the bullet's still in there.'

Dalton swore, but more at the inconvenience of it than anything else.

'Better get you to Ingalls, Bill,' Dick went on. 'Let Doc Selph take a look at it.'

Bill didn't want to risk that, but knew what might happen if he didn't. He'd seen wounds turn bad before, more than once, and it was never pretty. 'All right,' he managed. 'Help me up.'

Dick tried, but quickly gave up. 'You'll never make it tonight, Bill,' he concluded. 'You're already burnin' up with fever.'

'Well, we can't stay here,' muttered Dalton.

'We don't have to,' said Dick. 'We can head for Riley's place.'

Jim Riley ran a small ranch about a mile east of Lenora. It was the closest place to their position right then, and Riley was known to offer help and sanctuary to men who lived outside the law.

'All right,' Bill murmured reluctantly. 'Riley's place, it is.'

★　★　★

By the time they reached their destination — a small cattle ranch in poor repair — it was full dark. Hearing their approach, Riley — a big, grizzled man of about sixty — came out into the yard with a rifle across his barrel chest. Beside him was an unarmed man in his early twenties, who was holding a glass of milk in one hand.

'Who *are* you?' called Riley. 'Identify yourselves!'

'It's us, Jim,' called Dalton, riding into what little light spilled from the house's small tarpaper windows. 'We've had trouble. Doolin got hisself shot.'

Riley turned to the man with him. 'Gimme that there glass, an' help that feller inside.'

They got Bill stretched out on Riley's old truckle bed and then Riley peeled the blood-soaked sock off his foot and cleaned the heel, working deftly for such a big man. Bill stood the pain for as long as he could, then grated: 'Got any . . . whiskey, Jim?'

'Sure.'

Riley pressed a half-empty bottle into his hand. Although he'd never been much of a drinker, Bill took a long pull and coughed a little as the rye coursed through him. Then Riley took the bottle back and emptied what was left over his heel. The liquor stung like a hornet.

Finally the big man knelt and wrapped the injured foot as best he could with the cleanest strip of bandage he could find. 'Better get some rest now,' he advised. 'You've lost a lot of blood.'

By then Bill, looking pasty and heavy-eyed, was in no shape to do anything *but* rest. 'B-best . . . you fellers push on,' he told Dalton and the others. 'I'll join up . . . with you . . . soon as I can.'

'I'll stick around,' offered Jack. 'Take you into Ingalls first thing in the mornin'.'

'He might not be in any fit state to move that soon,' said Riley, scratching at his matted gray beard. 'You're welcome to stay, Jack, but it sounds to me like you fellers'd be better off makin' yourselves scarce for a while. Healy's not gonna quit that easy, not now he's lost men.'

'Jim's right,' said Riley's hired man, speaking for the first time. 'Anyway, I'll see that Mr. Doolin here reaches Ingalls, soon as he can ride again. Be proud to.'

The young man was lean almost to the point of starvation, with small, dark eyes set above prominent cheekbones. He wore a chevron mustache and had about him an air of sobriety that verged on the downright maudlin.

'This here's Roy Daugherty,' said Riley, finally thinking to introduce him. 'He's one of your own kind, boys. You could trust him with your life.'

Dick narrowed dark eyes at him. 'Now that I think on it, seems to me I've see you before,' he said cautiously. 'But back then you were called Arkansas Tom Jones.'

Daugherty — Jones — nodded. 'I won't deny it. I'm Arkansas Tom, an' proud of it.'

'Well, I hate to leave you like this, Bill . . . ' began Dick.

'But it's like Riley just said,' cut in Dalton, already heading for the door. 'We'd best make ourselves scarce. Come on, you boys.'

As an afterthought he paused in the doorway, looked back and added: 'Take your time mendin' Bill. I'm sure we'll all get along jus' fine without you.'

6

When Riley shuffled into what passed for his parlor the following dawn, he found Bill up and ready for travel. Though Bill felt like hell and looked about the same, there was no time to convalesce right then — he needed to get that bullet taken out and then get back to the cave-hideout at Beaver Creek before Dalton could turn the Oklahombres against him.

'Well . . . you know you're welcome to stay here just as long as it takes,' said Riley, scratching his chest through a stained red undershirt.

'I know it, Jim, an' I 'preciate it. But right now . . . well, right now I ain't got time on my side.'

'You're talkin' 'bout Dalton, I reckon,' Riley commented as he set about fixing breakfast. 'Lord, I seen hungry men in my time, but I seldom seen a hungrier one than that *hombre*. He wants to outshine his brothers somethin' fierce, don't he? And he'll do whatever it takes to get 'er done.'

'He'll *try*,' Bill replied.

'Well, you don't need to hear it from me, but I'll say it anyway,' said Riley. 'You watch that snake. First chance you get, you stomp him.'

After breakfast, Arkansas Tom saddled their horses and he and Bill set out on the thirty-mile ride to Ingalls. The early morning was cool, but give it another hour or so and they'd be cooking under a merciless sun.

'I was thinkin', Mr. Doolin,' Tom said after the first couple of miles. He now carried a Remington New Model Army .44/.40 at his belt, and looked a little more like the bad man he professed to be. 'I'd like to, ah, join up with you fellers, happen you think you could find a place for me.'

Feverish eyes constantly scouring their surroundings, Bill said: 'I thought you worked for Riley?'

'No, sir. He took me in when I needed it, an' I helped out best I could to repay him, but he always knew I wouldn't stay on forever.'

'Well, what the hell you want to join us for?'

''Cause there's safety in numbers, I guess,' Tom replied with a shrug. 'An' there's opportunities for a man to advance himself in such comp'ny as yourself.'

'Are you joshin' me, Arkansas Tom?'

'No, sir. I mean it.'

'Then you got me flummoxed. It's my understandin' that you come from right decent stock.'

'I do, sir. Fine, God-fearin' people. Hell, both my brothers are preachers, so you could say God's our stock-in-trade, an' me, I don't even drink, prefer the taste o' milk, always have. But, aside from that . . . well, I guess I was always cut from different cloth, an' as such a disappointment to my folks. Left home when I was fourteen, been alone an' on the drift ever since. But you wouldn't be takin' on any amateur, Mr. Doolin. I know my way around horses, cattle an' . . . well, I've had more'n a mite of experience in the, ah, bankin' business.'

Bill eyed him askance. 'Makin' more *withdrawals* than deposits, I'm thinkin'?'

Tom submitted to a rare chuckle. 'Yessir.'

'Well, no promises, Arkansas Tom, but we'll see how you . . . shape up.'

Tom scowled suddenly. 'You all right, Mr. Doolin?'

Bill nodded, but the face beneath his broad-brimmed black hat had flushed considerably. 'Just a mite . . . dizzy, is all. An' call me . . . Bill, will . . . you?'

'Yes, sir — uh, Bill. You just shorten rein a minute and take a little rest, now. Here, have a drink.'

Tom offered his canteen, and the water helped a little, but the pain of the wound and the heat of the day had worn Bill down faster than he'd thought possible.

Around the middle of the afternoon they finally reached their destination. Ingalls was a random scattering of sorry-looking wood-frame houses situated around a single, rutted street. The street itself was flanked by a collection of stores, saloons, a blacksmith's, livery stable and hotel. The hotel was the only two-story building Ingalls could boast, for it was still very much a town in the making — or so its inhabitants kept telling themselves. Settled during the Land Run of 1889, its population had yet to grow beyond a hundred and fifty, making it a poor relation to Stillwater, its near neighbor ten miles to the west.

By the time they entered town Bill was flagging noticeably, and if his flushed face was anything to go by, his fever had returned with a vengeance. As Tom angled them toward the Pierce O.K. Hotel, however, he seemed to come alive again. Edith's friend, Mary Pierce, ran the place, and Edith often stayed with her. It could even be she was here right now.

A couple of boys in patched, too-big coveralls were playing marbles on the boardwalk out front. They abandoned their game in order to watch the newcomers dismount, Doolin moving with effort and keeping off his left foot as much as he could. He and Tom tied up at the rack, then Tom helped Doolin up onto the warped boards. As he opened the door to allow Bill to hobble inside, he told the boys to quit gawping and go fetch Doc Selph.

The hotel lobby was small and dingy, its plank walls hidden beneath water-stained wallpaper that featured birds of plumage. Alerted by Tom's voice, Edith came out from a room behind the counter, a large, handsome woman of about forty behind her — Mary Pierce herself.

Edith's expression slackened when she saw Bill. Before she could ask the obvious question Tom said, addressing Mary: 'He caught one in the heel, Mrs. Pierce. Doc's on his way over.'

Edith quickly came around the desk to take Bill's other arm, and with Mrs. Pierce fussing about them, they somehow got him out of sight in the back room and onto an over-stuffed sofa beneath the curtained window.

'Doc'll need scissors an' hot water when he gets here,' decided Mrs. Pierce, and hurried away to fetch both.

As Edith examined him anxiously, Bill leaned back, eyes screwing shut with pain. 'When did it happen?' she asked.

'Last . . . night.'

'Last *night!*' She immediately turned to Tom. 'You should have fetched him here straight away!'

'Don't . . . blame Tom,' Bill husked. 'He wasn't even . . . there when it happened.'

Edith flustered. 'I'm sorry, Mr . . . '

'Arkansas Tom Jones, ma'am. Pleased to make your acquaintance.'

Turning back to Bill, Edith asked: 'Who did it to you, Bill?'

'Didn't . . . stop to take the . . . feller's name,' he replied. 'But he was ridin' with Frank Healy.' He broke off as the two boys appeared in the doorway.

'I thought I told you to go fetch Doc Selph?' said Tom.

'H-He ain't in,' said one of the boys. 'Mrs. S-Selph says he's over to Stillwater. Said Mrs. Hart's due any time now, and — '

'When'll he be back?'

'Not till tomorrow, she said.'

'Damn.'

The boys looked at Doolin. 'Are you gonna die, mister?' asked one of them.

''Course not!' said Mrs. Pierce, coming back from the kitchen with a towel over one chubby arm and an enamel bowl of steaming water held beneath her considerable bosom. 'Now, you boys get out of here. And keep your silence over this! There'll be fried apples for you if you do.'

Edith finished unwrapping the bandage. Bill's foot was caked with blood and had swollen to about twice its normal size. Gently, she started to bathe it with the damp towel, but as gentle as she was, Bill still winced at every touch.

'You think Sheriff Healy might come here, looking for you?' she asked.

'There's always the . . . chance.'

'Well, we'd better get you upstairs,' Edith said at last. 'Less folks know you're hurt, the safer I'll feel.'

'Ain't nobody around here gonna turn Bill in,' Mrs. Pierce reminded her.

'Maybe not. But — '

'Hush, woman,' said Bill. 'I'll . . . stay over Light's, same as always.'

'You can't! Not with your foot needin' to be — '

'Take the horses over to Ransom's,' Bill interrupted, his tone making it clear that he would brook no argument about it. 'Tell him to keep 'em hid there for a while.'

Biting back a response, she said softly: 'All right.'

'An' Edith . . . ?'

'Yes?'

'I'm sorry,' he said earnestly. 'For givin' you nothin' but grief, I mean.'

It grew very quiet in the room. Then she smiled at him and said: 'In sickness and in health, remember?'

There was something in the way she said it, in the secretive, knowing smile that accompanied the words, that started him thinking.

Tom frowned from one of them to the other. 'Is there anythin' you want to tell me, Bill?' he asked.

Bill shook his head tiredly. 'No,' he replied. 'But there . . . sure is someone I want you to *meet* . . . Edith Marie Doolin — my wife.'

* * *

While Tom and Mrs. Pierce helped Bill toward the back door, Edith went out onto the street, untied the horses and led them up toward the livery barn. To reach it she had to pass Ransom & Murray's Saloon, a small wooden-framed building on the corner of a side street, its front door and two windows facing onto main. A small ice house was tacked on at the rear, and the livery barn stood just south of it.

As Edith headed for barn, her attention was taken by a rider, coming in fast from the south. He looked as if he was going to ride straight through town without stopping, but when he saw Edith he suddenly yanked back on his reins and his paint pony slithered to a halt. Edith recognized him immediately as Little Dick West, one of the men Bill had recently brought into the gang. Small, lean and about thirty years old, he was the only member of Bill's gang who favored two guns, but right now his expression alone was enough to put her on her guard.

'Bill's around, ain't he?' he said, gesturing to Possum.

She nodded.

'Well, tell him Heck Thomas is less'n a mile behind me!'

Before Edith could react, he spurred the horse back to a gallop.

For a moment she just stood there, absorbing the news. Bill was in no fit state to make a run for it. If he tried that, Thomas — a marshal of fearful reputation — would catch him for sure.

Quickly she tugged the horses back into a walk and led them into Ransom's

Barn, where a short, squat man of about sixty was sitting on an upturned bucket in front of the stalls, polishing a bit. This was Fred Ransom — and the minute he looked up he saw the concern in her expression.

'Edith? What's — ?'

'If anyone asks, Mr. Ransom, you bought these horses from Bill over a week ago,' she said, a slight catch in her voice.

Ransom didn't need a diagram; he understood the situation immediately. As he took the reins from Edith he said: 'I got it. Come to think of it, I was standin' right on this very spot when Bill made me the sale.'

His broad wink made Edith feel better. She smiled her relief and then turned to hurry over to A. J. Light's open-fronted blacksmith shop, there to warn Bill and Arkansas Tom about Heck Thomas's imminent arrival.

7

Bent over his anvil and hammering shape into a horseshoe, big, muscular A. J. Light looked up as she entered. Without missing a beat, he gave a slight nod toward the rear of the shop.

Even as Edith hurried past him, a lean, long-legged man in his early forties walked his roan horse into town, the mild blue eyes beneath the brim of his pulled-low gray hat constantly on the move. He wore a neat tweed jacket over dusty black pants and a white shirt with a black string tie knotted neatly at his throat. Around his narrow hips he wore a gunbelt, in the tied-down holster of which sat a Remington New Model Army .44.

He drew rein outside the Pierce O.K. Hotel, stepped down with a single, fluid motion and went unhurriedly inside, his shadow spilling across the boys on the boardwalk, who had gone back to playing marbles.

Mrs. Pierce, seated behind the desk, knitting needles clicking busily in her hands, looked up as he came inside. At once the sound of the needles ceased. Betraying nothing of the sudden fear she felt, she greeted him with a seemingly warm: 'Why, Marshal Thomas — what a pleasant surprise.'

He wasn't fooled for a moment. Still, he removed his gray hat and nodded respectfully. 'Mornin', Mrs. Pierce.'

Henry Andrew 'Heck' Thomas had been born in Georgia and raised in Atlanta: his impeccable manners were as much a part of him as was breathing or blinking. A quietly authoritative man with carelessly-brushed sandy hair and an equally pale, untrimmed mustache, he'd turned his back on a career as a Methodist minister in order to pursue a more physical life, initially as a soldier in the late War of Northern Aggression. When his father became Atlanta's first city marshal back in '67, Heck had immediately signed on as his deputy. Distinguished spells as a railroad guard and an employee of the Fort Worth Detective Association had followed. And as his reputation grew, so he'd come to the attention of 'Hanging Judge' Isaac Parker, who had offered this tough man a tough job — as a deputy U.S. Marshal in Oklahoma Territory.

'How . . . how about some lunch, Marshal?' Mrs. Pierce went on, doing her best to sound as if nothing could please her more than having him around for any length of time. 'Be no trouble.'

'No thank you, ma'am.'

'A cup of coffee, then?'

'Can't stay but more'n a minute,' he replied, glancing toward the staircase. 'Miss Ellsworth around?'

Mrs. Pierce held his gaze for a moment longer than she should have, then said: 'I'm . . . afraid not. I sent her on an errand.'

Thomas looked her straight in the eye. She had the absolute conviction that he could see right into her, and sort truth from lie without even trying.

Then —

'Good morning, Marshal.'

Both turned as Edith came in off the street. She joined Mrs. Pierce behind the counter and said: 'What can we do for you, Mar — '

But Thomas had had his fill of this tired game they played. He said: 'You'll excuse me if I cut straight to the chase, Miss Ellsworth, but right now I have more pressing business with a feller name of Dick West. Since I was in the vicinity, however, I thought I'd stop an' tell you the news.'

'News?'

'That Bill's been shot.'

He waited for her reaction. It came as a single, slow blink. 'I'm sorry, Marshal, but . . . why would that concern me?'

'Well, it's no secret you're sweet on him.'

'That's ancient history, I'm afraid.'

'Is it, indeed? The way some folks tell it, you actually *married* him. In secret, of course.'

She held up her left hand. 'Well, as you can see, I don't wear any wedding band.' And she hadn't, for this very reason, ever since that March day in Kingfisher. She'd have to start soon, though, when the baby began to show.

'Well, as I understand it,' Thomas went on, 'Bill got hisself shot, and as I say, since I was passin' this way, I thought I'd — '

He broke off abruptly.

Unnerved and trying not to show it, Edith said: 'Uh . . . what is it, Marshal?'

He brought his eyes up to her face. 'I see you've hurt yourself,' he noted softly.

'I'm sorry?'

His eyes dropped fractionally, and when she looked down, she saw a small but fresh bloodstain on the front of her cheap brown dress.

Silence began to congeal until Mrs. Pierce said briskly: 'Oh, my, we'd better get that washed right out away. Excuse us, will you, Marshal? Chicken blood leaves an ugly stain if it's left to dry.'

'Chicken blood?' he repeated.

'That . . . that's what I was going to offer you for lunch,' said Mrs. Pierce. 'What we're having for our own supper, later on. Fresh chicken.'

She tried to hurry Edith through the door toward the kitchen, but Edith held her ground for another moment, looked as evenly as she could at Thomas and said: 'I'm obliged for the news, Marshal. But . . . well, Bill an' me got to fussing a while back, an' I . . . I reckon whatever understanding we had, it's over now.'

Beneath his sandy mustache, the near-imperceptible tightening of Thomas's lips showed exactly what he was thinking. She was lying. He knew it, but he had no real evidence to back it up, just gut feeling. And out here, you didn't call anyone a liar, least of all a woman, 'less you could prove it.

'I understand, Miss Ellsworth,' he said mildly. 'Well, good day, ladies.'

As soon as the front door closed behind him, both women sagged. They looked at each other, then hurried to the window to watch Thomas remount, turn his roan north and ride away — presumably, in pursuit of Little Dick.

'How could I have been so stupid!' Edith berated herself. She gestured to the bloodstain, said despairingly: 'Now he knows Bill's here for sure!'

'Maybe not, dear. Could be he believed us.'

Edith wasn't prepared to chance that. 'I'd better warn Bill. Just in case Thomas comes back and starts sniffing around.'

'All right. But stick to the back alleys. If Thomas *does* come back, I'll tell him . . . I'll tell him you've gone to wash your dress and change into a fresh one.'

★　★　★

Bill was sitting on the edge of a hard cot in one corner of the small room behind Light's blacksmith's shop when Edith appeared in the patched-curtain doorway. Catching the movement, he sat forward quickly, Colt in hand, and immediately winced at the pain in his foot.

'Uhn . . . *dammit!*'

Edith hurried over to him. The room was filled with old harnesses, blacksmith aprons, an assortment of dusty tools and some poor sticks of furniture. The only light entered through a tiny, dusty window beside the back door.

'He . . . gone?' asked Bill, referring to Heck Thomas.

'Yes, he's gone. But — oh, Bill, I think he knows you're here! In town, I mean.'

'What? How?'

She gestured to the bloodstain. 'He saw this, and mentioned it. I just froze up. Mrs. Pierce told him it was chicken blood, but I don't think he believed it.'

'Damn!' muttered Bill. 'Then I got to push on.'

'You're not in any *shape* to push on,' argued Tom. He had been seated on an upturned crate to one side of the doorway, nursing a glass of milk. ''Sides which, where would we go?'

' "We?" '

'Reckon I'll stick around,' said Tom. 'Leastways till you've decided whether or not I can join you fellers permanent.'

Edith said: 'It's risky, but I don't see that you've got much choice, Bill.' She thought a moment, then: 'He said he had more pressing business with Little Dick, but for all we know he's already on his way to round up help.'

'Could be,' agreed Bill. 'But to do that he's got to . . . head for Stillwater or Guthrie, and once he gets there he'll have to check in with the local law, get them to . . . help him raise a posse. After what happened with . . . Healy's boys, them local men won't exactly be champin' at the bit to sign up. My guess is he won't get back here till . . . tomorrow at the earliest. That's if he's comin' back at *all.*'

Tom nodded. 'All right. So we stick around as long as we dare for Doc to get back. If he don't get the lead out of your heel, you're finished anyway.'

'Thanks,' Bill muttered sourly.

'Oh, I'm a reg'lar ray of sunshine,' said Tom. He stood up, set his glass aside and headed for the doorway.

'Where're *you* goin'?' asked Bill.

Tom shrugged. 'Take a look around town,' he replied, and threw a wink in Edith's direction.

Edith smiled, knowing that he was going out to do no such thing. He was giving them a moment together, and moments like that were so few and far between that she appreciated Arkansas Tom Jones fiercely in that moment, for his loyalty to Bill, and his consideration for both of them.

★ ★ ★

It was a long night, and the birth Dr. Abraham Selph had to attend in Stillwater proved to be every bit as taxing as he'd expected. At last, with mother and child recovering from the ordeal in the good care of a local woman, he'd taken his payment, flopped down on the seat of his little back-to-back pony trap and allowed his horse to pick its own way back to Ingalls.

It was a little after dawn when he let himself into his cluttered office behind the meat market, and only a few seconds later that there came an urgent rapping at the door. Selph, a wiry little man of sixty, muttered irritably about there being no rest for the wicked, then called: 'I'm not here!'

The door opened and Edith and Tom helped Bill limp inside.

The minute he saw Bill, Doc forgot all about the coffee and pipe he'd been promising himself all the way back from Stillwater and said briskly: 'Get him up onto the table.'

They did so, after which Doc made a thorough examination of the wound, then sedated Bill with chloroform anesthesia and slowly, carefully removed the bullet.

Once the misshapen .30/.30 was resting in an enamel kidney dish, he cleaned the wound and bound it. By then Bill was starting to come round again. As Tom helped him sit up, Doc thrust a scarred set of crutches toward him.

'You'll be needin' these for a while.'

Edith helped him tuck a crutch under each armpit, then supported him as he stood, resting his weight on them and trying to keep his injured foot off the floor.

'Obliged, Doc,' he managed, looking hollow-eyed and feeling woozy. 'How long, ah, afore I can start . . . gettin' about under my own steam again?'

'Hard to tell,' said Doc. 'Several weeks, at least.'

'That long?'

'Bullet did a lot of damage, Bill. And bones need time to heal — lots of it. 'Specially if they're going to heal *right.*'

Something in his tone made Edith feel uneasy. She watched the doctor cross to the copper-lined sink, work the pump handle and then wash the blood off his hands.

'But it *will* heal?' she said. 'In time, I mean?'

'It *should.*'

'What does that mean?' asked Bill.

Selph looked at him. 'It'll never be as good as new,' he said. 'You'll limp on it for the rest of your life.'

Bill was silent as he took that in. It was bad news for any man, but worse still for one who only kept his freedom by keeping one step ahead of the law.

'Won't affect me ridin' at all?' he asked.

'Shouldn't do. Not once the bones've knit.'

Bill nodded. 'All right. Thanks, Doc.'

'Well, come back in a few days from now, if you can. Best if I check, make sure your heel don't take an infection.'

'That might be tricky,' said Bill.

'Then I'll come out to *you*.'

'I'll be holed up at the Rock Fort,' Bill said. Edith stiffened, for this was the first she'd heard of it. Before she could say anything, however, Bill stuck out his hand and shook with the physician. 'Thanks, Doc.'

8

Outside, Tom helped Bill climb into a buckboard they'd rented from Fred Ransom. Edith, watching concernedly, finally said: 'I'll go with you. To Rock Fort, I mean.'

He looked down at her, already hating his disability. 'Rock Fort's . . . no place for a woman.'

'What about Rose Dunn?' she countered.

Rose was the old-before-her-time sister of the five Dunn brothers. The Dunns — Bee, Calvin, Dal, George and Bill — ran a ranch not far from Ingalls, and operated a meat market in Pawnee, twenty-some miles south, where they sold the stock they rustled. He could understand Edith's misgivings. No one but a fool would ever trust the Dunns completely. Though none of them was actually wanted by the law, there were plenty of stories of folks stopping by their place for food and shelter who were never seen again. But Rock Fort, as they called their place along Council Creek, offered a degree of safety Bill didn't think he could find anyplace else right then.

'Three things about Rose Dunn,' he replied. 'One, she's just a kid — fifteen, at most. Second, she fancies herself as Bitter Creek's woman.'

'And third?' prompted Edith.

'Third,' he said, and hesitated just a moment before continuing, 'Rose Dunn ain't carryin' my son.'

The expression of surprise on her face told him he'd recognized that secretive, knowing smile of hers for exactly what it was — the knowledge that she was pregnant.

'How did you know — ?' she began.

'I jus' knew,' he said. 'That's all.'

'I got no secrets from you at all, have I?'

'Nary a one,' he said, and summoned a grin for her.

She looked up at him, wanting to say so much in that moment, and in the end saying only: 'I'll come see you soon as I can.'

'Well, you stay away for a while, just in case ... Thomas comes sniffin' around again. And if you *do* come out to Rock Fort, you make sure you're not followed.'

'I will.'

Tom cleared his throat. 'Better make tracks, Bill.'

Bill looked across at Doc. 'Be sure and look after her,' he called.

Doc draped a fatherly arm around Edith's shoulders. 'As if she were my own,' he promised.

As the wagon rattled away, Edith half-whispered: 'He's a good man, isn't he?'

'Better than most,' Doc agreed, and then gave her a squeeze. 'Be a good father, too, I 'spect.'

'Yes,' she muttered, suddenly remembering Heck Thomas. 'If they'll only give him the chance.'

Rock Fort wasn't much more than a poorly-maintained cabin built from spare lumber. Around a yard dotted with strutting chickens stood an equally decrepit barn, corral and storage shed. Tom wheeled the wagon into the yard, scattering chickens as he went, then braked outside the cabin and hurried around the stamping team so he could help Bill climb down.

As Bill got the crutches settled into his armpits, a good-looking young girl came swaggering hips-forward out into the hard sunlight, followed by two men who shared her part-Indian coloring — glossy, crow-black hair, skin the color of burnished copper and dark hazel eyes above pronounced cheekbones. The girl was Rose Dunn, sometimes known by her many admirers as Rose of the Cimarron. The other two were her brothers, shifty-looking George and simple-minded, always-grinning Dal.

''Afternoon, boys,' Rose called. She

wore a green boys'-size shirt with the top four buttons undone, and a pair of suede pants that hugged her like skin. When she saw the state Bill was in she asked: 'What happened — that ugly gal of yours finally kick you out of bed?'

Bill forced a smile while those around him chuckled at the sally. It seemed easy for everyone else to forget Rose was just a kid: for Bill it was impossible, and though he hated the brazen way she studied him, he was under no illusions. She was only interested in him at all because he was a conquest she hadn't yet made.

'Need a place to rest up for a while,' he said.

'You got it.'

'Thanks. Bee around? Or Calvin?'

Her eyes shuttled to a line of pines off to the northeast. 'Bee and Calvin — they're below with Red Buck an' Johnny Starr in the dugout.'

Bill nodded, thinking grimly, *Red Buck. She means Dalton's buddy, Weightman.*

'Thanks for the ride, Tom,' he said, and shook with the younger man. 'You still serious about joinin' the Oklahombres?'

'Yes, sir — uh, Bill.'

'Then you're in,' said Bill. 'Stick close to Ingalls, an' I'll see you again when I get through healin'.'

Still feeling like hell from his recent surgery, he propelled himself unsteadily across the yard and through the trees for maybe a quarter of a mile until he came to what appeared to be some kind of storm cellar dug into the side of a hill. Here he hauled open the plank door and awkwardly descended a short flight of steps to a second door below. Bee and Calvin heard him coming long before he reached it. Bee, the eldest, unbolted and then swung the door open, showing surprise when he recognized the newcomer.

'Well, if you ain't a sight!' he said. The likeness shared by the entire clan was remarkable, and hinted strongly at Indian ancestry. Bee was a tall, copper-skinned man with thick stubble and one eye that always seemed bloodshot.

He stepped back, opened the door a little wider and allowed Bill to enter.

What lay beneath the ground was not so much a dugout as a dark, dirt-smelling cave with double bunks on either side and a small fireplace cut into the rock down at far end. It appeared that Bee had been playing poker with three other men at a crudely knocked-together table in the center of what passed for a room. By the smoky light of two low-hanging kerosene lamps Bill recognized Bee's younger brother Calvin at once. He knew Johnny Starr only vaguely, and nodded a cautious greeting.

'Well, look who it is,' said the final man, Red Buck Weightman. He was tall, lean and somewhere in his middle forties, with a thick mane of fire-red, naturally wavy hair and a large steerhorn mustache. Like Alf Sohn, Red Buck was something of a mystery man. Bill did know that he'd once been arrested by Heck Thomas for stealing mules in the Cherokee Nation, but had escaped from the specially-modified railroad car before it could deliver him to prison.

'Dalton said you stopped a bullet,' he went on, his voice sounding like gravel on broken glass. 'Way he told it, you was finished.'

Bill inclined one shoulder. 'Wouldn't be the first time Bill Dalton made a mistake,' he said mildly.

'So what happened?' asked Bee, closing and bolting the door behind him. 'We all — '

Before he could say more, Red growled: 'You gonna play cards or gab all day, Bee?'

Bee scowled at him, but knowing better than to argue with a man who possessed such an evil temper, he merely shrugged and flopped back into the chair he'd so recently vacated.

His foot aching like hell, Bill thump-walked around the table and took the weight off on one of the bunks. Behind him, Red cursed and slapped down his cards, clearly a sore loser. One card fell off the table to land on the swept-dirt floor. He made no attempt to retrieve it, so Johnny Starr picked it up for him.

'Wanna sit in, Bill?' asked Calvin Dunn.

'No thanks.'

'We're only playin' for pennies.'

'No thanks, Cal.'

'Be playin' for *serious* money a few days from now,' Red Buck leered.

Bill frowned at him. 'How so?'

A heavy pause followed his question. The men at the table exchanged looks. Finally Bee said uncomfortably: 'Red here's been tellin' us Dalton plans to rob the bank at Caldwell. Way he tells it, the place is jes' spillin' over with money, an' — '

'Not Caldwell,' Bill said flatly.

Red Buck thrust his jaw forward. 'Oh?'

'No.'

'Why not?'

'Two reasons,' said Bill. 'One, Dalton

doesn't call the shots with the Okla-hombres, now or ever. Two, a good friend of mine has money in that bank — an' I don't rob from my friends.'

'You talkin' about Oscar Halsell, I guess?' said Red Buck.

'As you say.'

'But he won't lose nothin' from it. Insurance'll make good the bank's losses.'

'No deal,' said Bill, and there was steel in his tone now. He was hurt, he was tired and the outlaw life was start-ing to pall again. 'Oscar treated me like kin, taught me to read an' write, even trusted me to handle his payroll, an — '

' — an' you busted your back for him, so that makes things even,' said Red Buck. His grin was a knife-slash in his face as he went on: 'Any case, Dalton's runnin' things while you're all laid up, Bill. Whether you care for it or not, that's the way things are. An' we're gonna take that bank for every last dime!'

Bill said softly: 'Better not try it, Red.'

The heavy silence grew downright

oppressive. Something in Red Buck's dark eyes flattened out, and his right hand drifted oh-so-casually toward the Colt at his hip.

'Best you don't take that tone with me, Bill,' he warned. 'I don't cotton to it.'

Bill looked at him a moment longer, then said: 'Then do somethin' about it.'

Red did. But even as his hand dropped the last inch or so and his fingers folded around the grips of his handgun, Bill moved with equal speed, and to hell with the pain of it.

He brought one of his crutches up and around and slammed Red in the face with it. Red yelped, reared backwards with blood spraying from his smashed nose and went over, smashing his cheap-wood chair beneath him.

Bill came up as Red started to sit up again, planted the end of the crutch in the center of Red's chest and with his free hand drew his own pistol. It was cocked and aimed at Red's blood-smeared face even before the big man properly realized what had happened.

'Hey, now, Bill — ' began Calvin. He, like the rest of them, had leapt away from the table for fear of stopping a bullet.

Ignoring Calvin, Bill said: 'Listen up, Red. You're gonna pack up and get out of here right now. You're gonna ride for Beaver Creek and when you get there you're gonna deliver a message to Dalton for me. You hear that?'

'Sonofabitch!' Red swore. 'You broke my nose, dammit!'

'One tug on this here trigger and I'll break your mother's *heart,*' Bill reminded him, taking up first pressure. 'Now — you *hear* me, Red?'

Red Buck spat blood, nodded.

'Then you tell Dalton that *I* say what we hit and when we hit it. He don't care for that, you tell him he can take it up with me, personal, any time he likes. And tell him this, as well. He goes ahead and robs that bank at Caldwell, I'll *kill* him.'

Red managed: 'You're makin' a bad

enemy, talkin' that way.'

'Well, Dalton knows where to find me. And he knows I sure ain't goin' anywhere for a spell. Any time he fancies his luck, you tell him I'll be waitin'. Same goes for *you*, Red. You try mixin' it up with me again, I'll leave you for the crows.'

At last he took the crutch away from the other man's chest and limped back a pace. 'Now get the hell out of here,' he snapped. 'You're disturbin' my recovery.'

9

For Bill, the next seven weeks felt more like seven years. He did as much as he could to make the time pass, but at first there wasn't a whole lot he could manage, being laid up as he was. As the weeks progressed, however, he was able to do away with the crutches and get mobile all over again — especially when it came to avoiding Rose Dunn. But Doc Selph had been right. Try as he might, he could no longer walk without limping.

It soon became clear that Dalton had backed down over his plan to rob the bank at Caldwell. Bill had expected no less. But he knew the time was coming, faster than ever now, when he and Dalton would have to settle the bad blood between them once and for all.

In the meantime, he thought about Edith practically all day, every day, but never once regretted telling her to stay away. He knew Heck Thomas of old. If Thomas couldn't find him, he'd do the next best thing, and follow someone who *could*.

He thought about the baby, too: his *son*. Though they'd done their best to keep their marriage a secret, he'd known it would never remain so for long. Sooner or later word would slip out. And now that Edith had fallen pregnant, the truth was going to come out for sure.

Still, the weeks without seeing her weighed heavily upon him, and he grew moody and close-mouthed until one day, whilst sitting outside the dugout and taking the sun, he heard the distant rattle and squeak of a buckboard coming in from the south, and dared to hope that it might finally be her; that the time had come at last when she judged it safe to visit him.

He was right.

He hobbled through the trees to the ranch yard just as she halted her folks' buckboard outside the cabin, and she had never looked so good to him. She wore an ankle-length dress in cornflower-blue, and he was startled to see just how much she was now beginning to show the pregnancy, even beneath the Ramona frock coat she wore over it.

Alerted by her arrival, Rose Dunn stepped out into the sunshine, and the two women — separated by so much more than just five years in age — swapped a look that was anything but cordial.

'Hold on a minute, honey,' Bill called as Edith wound the reins around the brake handle and began to climb down. He held out his hands and helped her. 'Don't want you slippin' or hurtin' yourself — or our boy.'

She came into his arms and he kissed her hard on the mouth with no thought for where they were or who was watching. Rose looked on enviously, then said: 'Hello, Edith. Nice to see you're still able to get around.'

Her tone said exactly the opposite, and Edith knew it.

'Thank you,' she replied a little stiffly, and slipping an arm around Bill's waist added: 'Love for a man gives a woman great strength, you know.'

'I'm sure it does,' Rose agreed frostily. 'Trouble is, that kind of love don't always keep him warm at night.'

Bill felt Edith stiffen beside him and said hurriedly: 'It might, Rose — happen you could remember which man you were lovin' at the time.'

Rose's Indian-dark, young-yet-old face hardened and she said coolly: ''Scuse me.'

As she turned and went back into the cabin, Bill looked down at Edith's belly and asked when she'd last see Doc Selph.

'This morning,' she replied. 'Everything's all right. Doc says I'm doing just fine — and so is the baby.' Her smile was infectious. 'I think I felt him *or her* kick again today.'

'*Again?*'

'Oh, he — or *she* — never stops . . . and I *love* it.'

He was going to tell her how fine that was when he saw something in her expression that made him say instead: 'What is it, honey? What's wrong?'

Not replying directly, Edith said: 'Can we . . . take a walk?'

'Sure.'

He led her toward a nearby stream shaded by loblolly pine, where they were able to sit down on a fallen tree that was warmed by the filtered August sunshine. In the distance cattle bawled and lowed. High above them, sandpipers and orioles provided a pleasant song.

Still bothered by Edith's expression, Bill said again: 'What is it?'

She hesitated briefly, unsure how to say it, and while he waited for her to speak he saw that she'd started wearing her wedding ring again. Then: 'I . . . I'm probably just being foolish — but — '

'Go on . . . '

'I want you with me, Bill,' she said. 'By my side — not — not — ' Much as she didn't want to, she did it anyway; she looked off toward the cabin, and Rose. 'Not here with that . . . *creature.*'

'Rose? Oh, come *on* . . . you don't think — '

'Of course I don't! But — ' She shook her head almost irritably. 'I don't know what's wrong with me, maybe it's the way I am right now. I know you wouldn't . . . well, *do* anything . . . but . . . well, I guess a woman wants her man near her when she's going to have his child — '

'His *son.*'

She looked at him. 'Still so sure it'll be a boy?'

'Bet my boots on it,' he said.

She stared off at the stream, as if it held great interest for her. 'I know I'm asking a lot,' she said, almost to herself. 'I mean, I know it'll be more dangerous for you in Ingalls, but a lot of the boys are already there — have been for quite a while now, and — Oh, don't listen to me, Bill. I'm just being foolish — foolish and selfish, and — '

But Bill had heard enough. He reached over and silenced her with a kiss.

'I was gonna tell you later,' he said softly when they finally parted.

'Tell me what?'

'That when *you* go back today, *I'm* goin' with you.'

For a moment it was almost too wonderful to believe. Then, with little girl enthusiasm, she hugged him to her. 'I know I shouldn't be so selfish — '

'Selfish, hell. It's what *I* want as well, you know.'

'Still, it'll be risky.'

'Then we'll just have to do what we can to make it as risk-free as we can, won't we?' he replied.

But even as he said it, he had a bad feeling that was going to be easier said than done.

★   ★   ★

After saying his goodbyes to the Dunns later that afternoon, he gathered his gear and climbed awkwardly up onto the buckboard beside Edith. Taking the reins from her, he drove the wagon away without a backward look at Rose, who stood hipshot before the cabin, a look of longing that was almost pitiful on her face.

As town drew closer and afternoon moved toward suppertime, Bill felt his stomach start clenching. He was taking a hell of a risk; he knew he was. But Edith was right — his place *was* beside her as her time approached. Besides, he *wanted* to be there with her.

Ingalls hadn't changed a bit in the past couple of months, except maybe to die just a little bit more. As they entered town and drew level with Ransom & Murray's Saloon, he thought about the rest of the boys . . . and Bill Dalton, of course. If he was going to have a reckoning with Dalton, he wanted to choose the time and the place, and here, *now*, wasn't it. But he couldn't deny that he wanted to see the others again, and spread the word that he was back. Then he'd start thinking up a new job to keep them in business.

Curiously, that notion left him feeling vaguely depressed. For all its monotony, his time at Rock Fort had given him a chance to get used to a routine — of sleeping soundly at night with a roof over his head, of eating passable food at a table instead of always on the run, of not having to spend long days dodging badges or bullets. After that, did he *really* want to go back to the outlaw life?

Part of him said no. And yet another part — the greater part — knew that he'd miss it something fierce if he were to give it up; that was, if it were even *possible* for him to give it up.

Glancing at him and seeing the way he looked at the saloon, Edith thought she could guess the nature of his thoughts. 'Why don't you go in and say hello to the boys?' she suggested.

He drew rein and offered her a sheepish grin. Remembering that day at Doc Selph's, when he'd surprised her by saying he already knew about the pregnancy, he said now: 'I guess *I* got no secrets from *you*, either.'

'It's my condition,' she replied. 'Doc says it makes a woman almost halfway smart!'

*   *   *

On the boardwalk, he watched her drive off down the street toward the hotel, then turned, hitched at his gunbelt to get the hang of his Colt just right, and pushed through the batwings. The saloon was a small, dark room with a plank-and-barrel counter along one wall and a scattering of tables and chairs occupying what remained of the splintery board floor. Red Buck Weightman was up at the bar, talking to a tough-looking man in a black suit and derby hat. Both glanced around when Bill came inside, and Red's shoulders hunched instinctively when he recognized the newcomer.

Bill stared at him a moment, waiting to see how this would play out.

Everyone knew Red Buck was as mean as winter, and unlikely to forget the debt he felt he owed Bill. The only question was — would he attempt to collect on it *now*?

A long fifteen seconds ticked away. Red Buck glared unblinkingly at him. But then he forced himself to relax, turned his back with studied indifference and went on talking to his companion.

With a shallow sigh, Bill turned to a corner table, where some of the boys — Bitter Creek, Arkansas Tom, Tulsa Jack and Bill Dalton — had been playing poker with a small, wiry man of about thirty, who was also wearing a suit and string tie.

Bitter Creek Newcomb was the first man on his feet. 'Well, damn my eyes!' he roared, coming forward to pump Bill's hand enthusiastically. 'When the hell did *you* get in?'

'Just this minute,' Bill replied, focusing on Dalton now.

'All healed up?'

'About as healed as I'm likely to get.'

With a glass of milk within easy reach, Arkansas Tom was next to shake his hand, while Tulsa Jack grabbed an empty chair and set it down beside him.

'This here's Doc Roberts,' said Tom, indicating the thin man in the string tie. Roberts was a pale man with a small face and a long turkey neck. 'He's a surveyor for the railroad,' he continued, then gestured to the heavier-set man talking to Red Buck at the bar. 'That's his assistant, Orrington Lucas.'

'Railroad, eh?' said Bill, feeling uncomfortable around men he wasn't sure he could trust.

'Atchison, Topeka and Santa Fe,' supplied Roberts. 'We're here surveying for a new spur line. Pleasure to make your acquaintance, Mr, ahh . . . '

'Doolin,' said Tom. 'This here's Bill Doolin, Doc.'

Bill glanced down at him. 'I'd as soon not have my name tossed around.'

'You can relax around Doc,' said Tulsa Jack. 'He might be a railroad man, but he's got no axe to grind with us.'

'No, sir,' said Roberts. 'It's always been my experience that you find the *real* robbers in the board rooms.'

Bill shrugged and sat down. 'Well, deal me in, boys.'

Dalton had been gathering up the cards from the last game. 'You sure about that, Bill?' he asked, finally breaking his long silence. 'I figure you used up the last o' *your* luck when that bullet hit your heel instead o' your head.'

Bill subjected him to a long, flat stare before saying softly: 'Which bullet was that — the one fired by Frank Healy's posse man, or the one *you* thought about puttin' in me while I was runnin' for them rocks you'd holed up in?'

It went very quiet at the table.

'I don't know what the hell *that's* supposed to mean,' Dalton growled at last, clearly flustered.

Bill shrugged. 'Then just deal.'

Thin-lipped, Dalton did as he was

told. At the end he helped himself to a card. 'Dealer takes one.' His eyes shuttled to Bill. 'Your bet.'

Bill studied his cards momentarily, then threw money into the pot. 'Ten dollars oughta keep you tinhorns honest.'

That kind of money was too rich for Tom and Tulsa Jack. One after the other they threw their cards down with a resigned: 'Pass.'

'I'll see your ten,' said Bitter Creek, glancing up at the lewd painting on the wall behind the bar. 'An' raise you twenty for the gal with the big titties on the wall over there!'

He added money to pot and then raised his whiskey glass in salute to the painting.

Doc Roberts threw down his cards. 'Too rich for a poor railroad man,' he said.

Bill took another look at his hand, weighed his decision briefly, then: 'See the ten, see the twenty bump . . . an' raise you fifty more.'

The bet hit Dalton like a slap in the face.

'*Fifty!*' he breathed. 'Where the hell you get fifty dollars from?'

'Man don't get much chance to spend his money when he's been holed up for two months.'

'Yeah, but *fifty* dollars . . . '

'Don't you have it?' Bill asked innocently. Almost immediately, however, he appeared to remember something. 'No, course you don't. You never *did* get to the bank at Caldwell, did you?'

Dalton looked at him over his cards. His eyes were as lusterless as ever, but deep in their depths was a flicker of hatred.

A moment more, and then he slapped his cards facedown and swore. 'Fold,' he muttered.

Bitter Creek studied his own cards a little more closely. 'Reckon I'll jes' have t' see you.'

He added fifty dollars to pot, and watched as Bill lay down his cards.

'Three tens,' said Bill.

Bitter Creek snorted and tossed in his own cards. 'Beats my two pair!' But he laughed as he said it. 'Damn you, Bill, why couldn't you have stayed at Rock Fort for another week or two? I was jus' beginnin' to clean up around here!'

'Rock Fort?' asked Roberts.

Bitter Creek was about to reply when Bill, raking in the pot, said sharply: 'Just a place I know.'

With a nod, Doc Roberts shoved his chair back and stood up, gesturing for his companion, Lucas, to join him. 'Well, in that case that's me done for today, gentlemen,' he said. 'Thanks for the company.'

'Leavin' kinda early, ain't you?' growled Dalton.

'Got some packing to do. I'm heading back to Guthrie in the morning.'

'Why so soon?'

The surveyor frowned, suddenly not liking Dalton's tone. 'We've been here almost a month, Mr. Dalton — '

' — most of which time you've spent

takin' my money.'

'Yessir,' agreed Roberts. 'And passing it right along to Mr. Newcomb and Mr. Blake here, both of whom are better with a deck than I am. But now the time has come for me to deliver my preliminary report on the feasibility of the proposed spur line.' He looked from one man to the next, ended with: 'Well, pleasure meeting you, Mr. Doolin. Gentlemen.'

Roberts and Lucas left the saloon and started down toward the hotel.

'Sonofabitch!' muttered Dalton.

10

That evening, after Mary Pierce had welcomed him back as if he were a long lost son, Bill and Edith dined together at the hotel. The only other patrons in the small dining room just off the lobby were Roberts and Lucas, who were sitting a few tables over, enjoying after-supper cigars. Bill played with more food than he ate, a fact that didn't go unnoticed by Edith.

'What's wrong?' she asked.

'Nothin',' he replied moodily. 'Just ain't hungry, is all.'

'You're good at a lot of things, Bill,' she said. 'But lying's not one of them.'

Some of the tension left him. 'It's just . . . aw, forget it.'

'No. You get it out of your system, whatever it is.'

'Well . . . this ain't no life to bring a child into, Edith. I mean, me sleepin' over at Light's, you here, upstairs, and the both of us slinkin' around like dogs in the night.'

At a loss as to how best to react, Edith settled for: 'What else can we do?'

'I don't know. I got to think on that, an' pretty damn' fast, too. That baby's gonna be here any day.'

'We could go somewhere else,' Edith suggested. 'Some place far away, where no one knows us.'

'Where?'

'New Mexico? California? I mean, why couldn't we? What's to stop us?'

'Money, for one thing. With this foot of mine, I ain't stole a dollar in nigh on two months. An' you're not goin' too far right now, not in your condition.'

'I'm all right. Doc Selph says I'm strong as an ox.'

'Winter's comin' on, too,' he muttered. 'Be just our luck to get caught out in the middle of nowhere, an' you havin' the baby afore it's time — '

He noticed then that Roberts and

Lucas had fallen quiet, and wondered if they were trying to eavesdrop. Even as he glanced at them, however, they quickly nodded politely, then went back to talking. Bill stared at them for another moment, then returned his attention to Edith.

'First thing I got to do, soon as my foot's healed proper, is get some money. Then, once the baby's born, an' can travel, we'll head out of here — go someplace I ain't wanted. We could maybe buy a little spread, an' raise our son so he don't feel ashamed of his ol' man's name.'

It was a long speech by Bill's standards, but when he finished it was rewarded by a glowing smile from Edith. Reaching across the table to place one of her hands over his, she said: 'Bill, if only we could.'

'We can. An' we *will*, too. You jus' wait an' — '

He broke off again as Roberts and Lucas rose and walked past them on their way out, each man touching his hat politely to Edith.

'Evenin', Miss Ellsworth — Mr. Doolin.'

As soon as the surveyors had left the room, Bill leaned forward and hissed: 'What do you know about them two?'

'Just that they work for the Santa Fe . . . that they're awful polite and don't bother anyone. Mrs. Pierce says she wishes she had a hotel full of their kind, instead of — '

' — the likes of me, eh?' he finished grimly.

'That's not true, and you know it! Why, Mrs. Pierce thinks you're one of the kindest, most gentle men she's ever known. An' if it means anything to you . . . so do I.'

Abruptly he shed years with a grin. 'Then maybe it's about time I started livin' up to my reputation,' he said.

★　★　★

Doc Roberts sat in the small room he'd been sharing with Orrington Lucas for

114

the past four weeks, lamp turned low and deep in thought. Over by the door, Lucas stood watching the hallway outside. Presently both men heard the sound of footsteps climbing the stairs. A moment later Bill and Edith appeared, arm in arm. Bill saw his wife to the door of her room, where she said: 'I hope you realize, Mr. Doolin, that I don't ordinarily allow strangers into my room.'

Playing along with her, Bill said: 'Oh, I do, ma'am. An' I appreciate you makin' this exception, believe me.'

As he finished speaking, he slapped her on the butt, making her giggle. They both entered her room and the door closed softly behind them.

Lucas closed the door and turned to Doc, his shadow stretching huge and misshapen up the wall behind him.

'Ain't that cute,' he said.

Doc gave a preoccupied nod to show that he'd heard. Lucas joined him at the window and together they stared down into the dark, empty street for a few moments.

'What's up?' Lucas asked when Doc remained silent.

'Nothing,' said Doc. 'Just can't believe he showed up when he did, that's all. Just walked right in as bold as brass. I was starting to think we'd been sent out here on a fool's errand.'

'Well, he's here, all right. Bill Doolin himself! And from the sound of things, he's not going anywhere any time soon. Which means we've got most all of the rats caught in the same trap.'

Doc nodded morosely.

'Well, don't look so happy about it!' Lucas admonished. 'It's what we've been working towards, isn't it?'

'Sure it is. But it's kind of sad to think that Doolin's kid won't ever know its pappy, don't you think? I mean, he struck me as a decent enough feller, his heart in the right place.'

'Don't let all that sweet talk downstairs fool you, Doc,' said Lucas. 'Like Marshal Nix says, Doolin's no different from the rest of this scum! Ain't a-one of 'em wouldn't cut his own mother's throat for a sack of nickels!'

But Roberts remained unconvinced. He was a married man himself, with two small children. That gave him a perspective that Lucas, a confirmed bachelor, sorely lacked.

As if to prove it, Lucas added harshly: 'You just wait. You'll soon see his true colors when we come back here an' wipe out this rats' nest — you mark my words!'

11

As the sun rose slowly on the first day of September, it illuminated the bewildering array of wagons and tents that filled the Pawnee Hills as far as the eye could see. Here and there tattered flags fluttered from crude or listing flagpoles, as did homemade banners that read CHEROKEE STRIP OR BUST!

Although there was still two weeks to go before the Cherokee Strip Land Run got underway, it was already starting to look as if demand would outstrip supply by a wide margin. It was impossible to estimate numbers with any certainty, of course, but the fourth so-called 'land run' the government had organized in Oklahoma had so far attracted well in excess of 100,000 would-be settlers. With more than 6.5 million acres up for grabs, it was to be the biggest land run yet, but it was doubtful that even that much land could hope to accommodate so many boomers.

As the sun climbed higher, a Murphy wagon rattled across the flats below the sprawling tent-town, its driver — Jim Masterson, brother of the more celebrated Bat — paying it no mind.

He had business elsewhere.

Urgent business.

Hidden beneath the patched tarpaulin strung over the wagon bows were four deputies and a deputy marshal, all of whom were loaded for bear — that was, armed to the teeth and ready for the fight of their lives.

When the last of the tents and wagons had fallen behind them, Deputy Marshal John Hixon informed his deputies: 'All right, keep it quiet back there and get yourselves set. I figure we got about less than a mile to go now.'

History was in the making.

★   ★   ★

In an upstairs room at the Pierce O.K. Hotel, Mrs. Pierce placed the back of one hand on Arkansas Tom's forehead and was relieved to find it cool to the touch. Twenty-four hours earlier, the young Missourian had come down with what had looked like the flu, but there was just one problem with that. This wasn't flu season. Oh, he'd shown all the right symptoms — fever, sweating, headache, back pain and general weakness — but there was something about the nature of the illness that had made Mrs. Pierce feel uneasy.

She'd called for Doc Selph, and to her surprise he'd diagnosed milk fever.

'I've seen enough cases of it in my time to recognize it for what it is,' he told her when she asked if he was sure. 'Does the feller like milk?'

'He doesn't drink much else,' Bill had supplied, hovering worriedly in the background.

'Then that's what it is,' Doc confirmed with a nod. 'He's drunk a spoilt batch and now he's got to fight off all the bacteria it contained.'

Now, at Mrs. Pierce's touch, Tom, his face almost as white as the pillow upon which he was resting, began to stir sluggishly. Behind them, the door opened and Bill limped in as quietly as he could.

'Is he any better?' he asked softly.

She nodded. 'Fever broke around two o'clock this morning.'

'And you nursed him through the whole thing.'

She shrugged, as if it were of no great consequence.

'Well, I appreciate it, Mary. He's a good man, is Tom. More'n that, he's a *friend.*'

Again Arkansas Tom stirred, and this time, when they looked down at him, they found him looking right back at them.

'How're you feelin', pard?' asked Bill.

'Like I'll sure think twice before I drink *milk* again,' Tom replied weakly.

Bill reached down and squeezed his shoulder. 'You'll live, I reckon.' Then he turned his attention back to Mrs. Pierce.

'You look beat, Mary. I'll have Edith come up and relieve you for a spell.'

She nodded, but Bill only got halfway across the room before Tom called his name. Bill turned back.

'What is it?'

Tom said: 'Don't go plannin' nothin' without me, you hear?'

'I won't,' Bill replied, adding with a grin: ' . . . Oklahombre.'

★　★　★

'Here they come,' hissed Deputy George Cox.

Deputy Dick Speed tossed his cigarette away and tried unsuccessfully to put a bridle on his rising anger. 'About damn' time!' he muttered.

He had driven a wagonload of deputies in from Guthrie the previous evening and parked the vehicle here behind a disused shack on the farthest edge of town. They'd been due to meet with Deputy Marshal Hixon's contingent at midnight, the plan being to take the Oklahombres while they slept.

There was just one problem. Hixon must have been delayed, because the night had passed without any sign of him — until now.

Speed watched sourly as Jim Masterson drew his wagon to a halt. Hixon and his men jumped down and perfunctorily, Hixon offered his apologies.

'Never mind,' said Speed, a cock-bantam of a man with a clean-shaven, rubbery face. 'You're here now.'

'So what's the position?' asked the deputy marshal, studying the dozing town and its layout.

Speed hooked a thumb toward a big, tough-looking man in a town suit. 'This is Orrington Lucas,' he said. 'It was him an' Doc Roberts who've been stakin' the place out, waitin' for Doolin to show his face.'

'I *know* who he is,' Hixon said testily. He looked at Lucas. 'Well?'

'They're in the saloon yonder. Dalton, Newcomb, Clifton, Red Buck

Weightman and Tulsa Jack Blake.'

'What about Doolin?'

'Doolin was with 'em at the saloon, but left a while ago and walked back to the hotel. I suspect he was goin' to check on Arkansas Tom Jones.'

'Why? What the hell's wrong with *him?*'

'Took sick, yesterday, just after Doc Roberts set out for Guthrie. In his bed at the hotel.'

Hixon chewed at his bottom lip. He was a big, broad-shouldered man of forty-five, with a thick waist that seemed to get thicker with every passing day. After a moment he said softly: 'I don't like it. I think we need reinforcements.'

Jim Masterson was incredulous. '*What?*'

'There's five of them in that saloon and Doolin still to rejoin 'em, and every man-jack there'll fight to the death before he'll surrender. A more sizeable show of force might change their thinking.' He gestured to one of the six deputies who'd arrived with Speed. 'What's your name, mister?'

'Lauson,' said the man.

'All right. Go rent yourself a horse from that livery down there, and ride for Stillwater. Tell 'em we need more men here, pronto.'

'We wouldn't need more men if you'd turned up on time,' Speed muttered as Lauson trotted away. 'We could've done this thing with no risk to ourselves.'

Hixon squared his big shoulders belligerently. 'Well, contrary to what you might've heard, these here Okla-hombres ain't the only business I got to occupy me. Now, the rest of you, fan out and find yourself some cover. Doolin's men ain't about to go far, but if they do, I want you fellers there to stop 'em.'

* * *

On his way back to the saloon to tell the others the good news about Arkansas Tom, Bill spotted a local lad by the name of Dell Simmons watering his father's wagon team at the public trough beside the blacksmith's shop and impulsively flicked him a coin. Dell caught it, grinned and nodded his thanks.

The boy had no way of knowing he would never live long enough to spend it.

* ★ ★

As the town started coming to life around them, Deputies Dick Speed and Tom Hueston entered A. J. Light's place from the rear and Hueston pressed his .45 up under the startled blacksmith's heavy, bearded jaw.

'Don't move, an' don't say a word,' hissed Hueston, whose brother Hamilton was also one of the posse men. 'This is law business, so you just mind your manners an' everythin'll be jake.'

Tired and scratchy-eyed from a night's worth of hanging around, Speed ghosted through the blacksmith's shop with a Winchester in his fists until he reached the entrance, from which he could see the saloon. Though he didn't know it, he'd just missed seeing Bill enter the place, but was in time to see another man come outside and check on his horse, which was tied to the rack out front. He frowned, trying to place the man but unable to do so.

A youngster was watering a wagon team at the nearby public trough. Speed edged out into the watery new-day sunshine and said in an undertone: 'Hey, kid. Who's that feller over yonder?'

Dell Simmons looked around and, seeing no reason to match Speed's tone, called back: 'That's Bitter Creek Newcomb.'

On the other side of the street, Bitter Creek heard his name spoken and looked up. He saw Speed standing there with a rifle in his hands and jumped to the obvious conclusion.

'Dammit!'

At once he grabbed for his Winchester and wrenched it from its saddle scabbard. Speed, seeing the move, took a pace out into the sunshine, slammed the stock of his own rifle to his shoulder and fired first.

The bullet smashed into Bitter Creek's rifle, deflected off the magazine and hit him in the crotch. Bitter Creek screamed, dropped his weapon and stumbled backward, bent double. Speed, deciding to press his advantage, came further out into the street, jacking a fresh round into the breech as he did so.

Before he could fire it there came a shattering of glass from the direction of the hotel. Speed twisted toward the sound, saw someone at a smashed window on the second floor and immediately raised his rifle with the intention of again getting in the first shot.

Arkansas Tom wasn't about to let that happen.

Though still sick to his stomach, he'd been quick to react to the first blast of gunfire. Pushing Edith aside when she tried to restrain him, he'd staggered to the window, smashed it and now steadied his Remington .44/.40 on the frame before squeezing off a round. The slug punched Speed in the chest and flung him hard against the side of the blacksmith's shop.

Speed was dead before he hit the dirt.

★　★　★

As Edith joined Tom at the window, she saw that chaos had claimed the town. Locals were running everywhere, their only thought now to get away from all the gunfire. Downstairs, Mrs. Price came out of the hotel, snatched the two marble-playing boys outside by their arms and hauled them into cover. With no further choice in the matter, Hixon and the rest of his deputies broke cover and immediately started shooting wildly in the direction of the saloon.

★　★　★

Bitter Creek, his body burning with the pain of his groin-wound, somehow managed to stagger to his horse, Old Ben, and mount up. Jim Masterson quickly threw himself behind a blackjack tree that was too skinny to provide much cover, and threw a shot at him. It missed.

For valuable seconds Bitter Creek swayed in his saddle, dizzy from pain, then jabbed his spurs into Old Ben's flanks. The animal took off at a gallop, headed southeast out of town.

Up ahead, two deputies ran out into the middle of the rutted roadway and started shooting at him. With a curse, Bitter Creek hauled back on his reins and Old Ben swung to the left and galloped into, and through, the livery stable. Seconds later horse and rider exploded out the rear exit, headed for timber — and safety.

★   ★   ★

Tom Hueston came charging out of the blacksmith shop, snap-aimed and sent a shot after Bitter Creek just moments before he vanished into the stable. It missed and struck an old man instead, and he dropped to the ground, howling and clutching one arm.

As more bullets bounced off the iron pump beside the trough, the horses Dell Simmons had been watering tore free of his grip and charged off up the street — directly into a scared ten-year-old girl, who'd been trying to bolt for cover.

★　★　★

In the saloon, Bill and the others began to smash windows and return fire as the deputies set about turning the front of the saloon into matchwood. In the first volley Ransom, who owned the place, and Murray, his bartender, had been hit and wounded. Now both men lay behind the crude bar, trying to doctor themselves as best they could, and moaning at the agony of their wounds.

As he thumbed back the hammer and tried to find a target, Bill thought about Edith. He'd left her with Tom; she should be safe enough. But what if she came out onto the street, tried to make it down here to the saloon to be with him? What if — ?

He stopped that line of thought right where it was, knowing it would serve no useful purpose. Edith would stay put . . . he hoped.

He yelled to no one in particular: 'We gotta get out of here, fast! We tarry overlong an' they'll get around behind us!'

'What about Tom?' asked Tulsa Jack.

Bill hesitated, remembered what he'd told Mary Pierce.

He's a good man, is Tom. More 'n that, he's a friend.

'We'll have to leave him,' yelled Dalton. 'Shape he's in, he couldn't ride right now, even if we could reach him.'

Bill wanted to dispute that, but knew it was true. Like it or not, Tom would just have to take his chances. But Bill felt something inside him die just at the thought of it.

Around them, glass continued to shatter as bullets chopped up the back bar shelves, shattered the fly-specked mirror and tore the painting of the gal with the big titties to shreds. Several more bullets slammed into the frame of the building, sounding more like lead shot on a tin roof. Another stray bullet hit one of the lanterns hanging from the rafters, and the men beneath it were showered with broken glass and kerosene.

Red Buck lurched to his feet and ran, bent double, toward the back door. The minute he jerked it open he was greeted by a flurry of gunshots.

'Dammit!' he cursed, hastily slamming the door shut again. 'We 're too late! The bastards've already got us surrounded!'

12

Tom Hueston broke cover and started running down the street to join his companions. Seeing him go, Arkansas Tom clenched his teeth against a sudden wave of nausea and sent two shots after him. Both of them hit, stopping Hueston dead in his tracks and making him turn a bizarre kind of pirouette. He dropped his .45 and followed it to the dirt, landing in an untidy heap.

He squirmed for a while, muttering the same thing over and over again until, quite suddenly, he died.

'I'd like . . . to see the man who . . . shot me . . . I'd like to . . . see the man who . . . shot me . . . '

★ ★ ★

Hunkering behind the public trough, where he'd taken cover when the shooting started, young Dell Simmons finally gave in and started to sob. He'd never been so scared in his life, and knew he had to get off the street and under cover if he was to avoid the same fate as the little girl who'd been killed by his runaway team.

Screwing up his courage, he got his legs under him, then bolted for the blacksmith's shop.

It was no more than four yards away. He should have made it easily. But across the street from him, one of Hixon's deputies caught the blur of movement he made and decided that he must be one of the gang, trying to escape.

Before Dell could reach the safety of Light's, the deputy snap-aimed and fired at him. The .56 caliber bullet whacked Dell up against the plank wall, where he teetered for a long beat, then fell lifeless to the ground.

It was only then that the deputy saw his mistake.

He turned away from the street, folded over and threw up.

★ ★ ★

Reaching a decision, Bill raised his voice above all the gunfire and said: 'Our best bet's through the front door!'

Dalton looked at him wide-eyed. 'You're crazy! They'll cut us down the minute we — '

Ignoring him, Bill checked his loads, then said: 'I'll go first, make a run for the livery. Once I'm there — '

'You won't *reach* the livery!' snapped Dalton. ''Case it's escaped your attention, you're a damn' cripple, Doolin!'

'Once I'm *there*,' Bill continued through set teeth, 'I'll give you fellers coverin' fire an' you come runnin'. We'll saddle up fast as we can and then get the hell out of here.'

The others muttered or nodded agreement. The atmosphere was heavy with sweat and fear.

'You better not run out on us,' said Dalton.

Bill hesitated to one side of the bullet-chewed batwings. 'You got no worries there,' he replied. 'I ain't like *you*, Dalton.'

The men took up places by windows or overturned tables and got ready to give him covering fire.

'Ready?' asked Dick.

'As I'll ever be.'

'Awright, you fellers . . . ready, Bill . . . *go!*'

Sucking a deep breath, Bill crashed out through the batwing doors, Colt punching lead at the lawmen across the street. Dalton and the others immediately started laying down covering fire.

Bill slipped a little, cursed his infirmity, then turned and sprinted for the stable. Crouched behind a barrel directly opposite, Doc Roberts, who'd returned to town with Hixon's contingent, sighted along the barrel of his Winchester and prepared to blow Bill to hell.

He tracked his limping target, his finger taking up first pressure on the trigger. One shot, that's all, and Doolin would *be* history even as Doc himself *made* it.

His finger whitened on the trigger.

Do it . . . do it . . .

But then he remembered what he'd told Lucas, up in their hotel room.

It's kind of sad to think that Doolin's kid won't ever know its pappy, don't you think? I mean, he struck me as a decent enough feller, his heart in the right place.

Doc cursed himself and his soft nature. Hell's fire, it was kill or be killed out here right now! And yet —

He eased back off the trigger . . . and allowed himself a brief smile as Bill vanished into the stable, unharmed.

*   *   *

Dalton glanced at his companions. 'We're up next, boys,' he said, his voice sounding scratchy in his ears.

There was a tense moment as he did his best to keep an eye on the front of the stable as bullets whipped through the shambles that had so recently been a saloon.

'The sonofabitch . . . ' he breathed after a moment. And then: 'I *knew* it! *The sonofabitch's run out on us!*'

Then Bill appeared around the half-open stable doorway and he was firing the Winchester he'd just drawn from his saddle scabbard, lever-fire, lever-fire, lever-fire —

'The *hell* he's run out on us!' cried Tulsa Jack. 'Come on, let's *go!*'

With the others crowding his heels, he burst out into the violent morning and started legging it for the stable. Knowing he had to salvage something from this mess, Deputy Marshal Hixon came around the edge of a stalled wagon and emptied his six-gun at the group. One bullet caught Dick; he staggered and quickly slapped a hand to his neck.

Blood started flowing from between his fingers.

He collapsed, Hixon's for the taking — until Arkansas Tom drew a bead on him from the hotel window and sent him scurrying back behind the wagon.

139

Meanwhile, Tulsa Jack dragged Dick back to his feet and hauled him into the stable. There, while he and Dalton kept the posse busy, Bill and Red Buck hastily saddled their horses. Trembling with reaction, Dick clumsily stuffed a kerchief against his neck and tried to staunch the flow of blood.

When the animals were ready to ride, Bill and Tulsa Jack helped Dick to mount up. Dalton and Red Buck were too concerned with their own safety to worry about anyone else. Ramming his heels into Possum's flanks, Bill yelled: *'Ride!'*

★   ★   ★

Crouching at the corner of the ice house that adjoined the stable, Deputy Lafe Shadley was just waiting for the Oklahombres to show themselves so that he could grab a little glory.

The second they exploded through the rear doors, he rammed the stock of his Winchester into his hip and fired from the waist. His first shot missed. His second blew the jaw off Dalton's rearing horse.

The horse spun, threw its rider, and Dalton hit the ground a second but no more before his animal. Bill and the others immediately returned fire. Shadley dodged back out of sight. Then Red Buck, Tulsa Jack and the barely-conscious Dynamite Dick were heading for the trees — and escape — at a gallop.

For just a moment Bill almost went after them. But he couldn't leave a man behind, not even a worthless sonofabitch like Dalton. Cursing himself for a fool, he turned Possum and angled toward Dalton, who was now clambering unsteadily back to his feet. When he was close enough, Bill kicked one foot free of the stirrup and yelled: *'Here!'*

Dalton didn't need any urging. But even as he toed in and made to swing up behind Bill, Bill saw Shadley appear at the corner of the ice house again, Winchester to his shoulder now.

He bawled: *'Hang on!'* and then kicked Possum to speed.

The animal bore down on Shadley. Shadley froze, startled by the sheer unexpectedness of the charge. As they drew closer, Bill saw his eyes saucer — and then Shadley finally had the presence of mind to throw himself to one side, out of the animal's path.

The deputy lost his footing, dropped his Winchester and belly-flopped in the dust, now well and truly out of the fight. But as they rode on past, Bill felt Dalton hip around a little behind him, chanced a quick sideways glance, saw the other man thrust his .45 to arm's length, then thumb-cock and fire it again, again, again.

The three bullets slammed into Shadley even as he stumbled back to his feet. The force of impact picked him up and threw him down again six feet from where he'd been standing.

Bill went numb. Then: *'What the hell did you do that for!'*

'He tried to kill us!'

'*There was no call to gun him down, damn you!*'

But this was neither the time not the place to debate it. Hating Dalton with a passion he hadn't even guessed he could possess, he jabbed Possum some more and the horse surged on toward the trees, gamely carrying the weight of two.

★   ★   ★

The Battle of Ingalls, as it would eventually come to be known, was over. Arkansas Tom stopped sniping after his companions lit out, and under threat of being blown to Kingdom Come by Jim Masterson, who fetched a stick of dynamite from the wagon he'd driven in on, he surrendered shortly thereafter.

In foul mood, and just a tad unnerved by the awful silence that suddenly claimed the town, Hixon huffed along the alleyway between the stable and the ice house, a few of his remaining deputies following in a hushed knot behind him. Out on the street they heard Hamilton Hueston, who had elected to stay beside the body of his brother, Tom, begin to weep.

Hixon shook his head, feeling dazed by the fight and how it had gone so disastrously wrong. The Oklahombres were gone, and all he had to show for it was three dead deputies, two dead locals and Lord alone knew how many wounded.

With no saddle horses of their own, there was no way they could give chase — even supposing they could catch up with Doolin's bunch. Those sons knew these hills better than they knew their own faces. They'd run rings around him and his deputies, and Hixon wasn't sure he could stand the humiliation of that, not coming so close on the humiliation of . . . of . . . this.

Irritably he stabbed a finger down at Shadley. 'He won't last long in this heat,' he said. 'Pick him up. We'll take him and the others back to Guthrie.'

And as he said it he thought: *God, I'm going to pay for this. If Marshal Nix doesn't hang my butt out to dry over it, Judge Parker certainly will.*

13

U.S. Marshal Evett Dumas 'E.D.' Nix sat back in his wood-paneled, neat-as-a-pin office overlooking Guthrie's busy Oklahoma Avenue, and surveyed his three visitors for a long, heavy moment. Then:

'Gentlemen,' he said in his distinctive Kentucky accent, 'I think you know why I've summoned you here.'

Nix had come to the Twin Territories two years earlier and set himself up in business, at which he'd quickly prospered. Of average height and build, with wavy, center-parted brown hair and an impressive handlebar mustache, the thirty-two-year-old had raised eyebrows when Judge Parker had sworn him in as U.S. Marshal for Oklahoma Territory just eight weeks earlier. His critics had claimed he was too young for such high office, and in looks Nix did indeed appear boyish, with his affable smile and seemingly innocent blue eyes. But he was also known to have a clear, cool head, a refreshing independence of thought and a quiet, unshakable confidence in himself. Furthermore, he had come from a family of peacekeepers; his father had served as a deputy sheriff, his uncle as a county sheriff.

Determined to justify his appointment, Nix had entered the halls of justice just like any other new broom; ready to sweep clean. The Twin Territories were a haven for the lawless. Cattle thieves, horse thieves, whiskey peddlers and men on the run were all drawn to its vast wilderness, knowing they would be largely safe from interference by such authorities as there were.

At first, it had been hoped that by opening the Cherokee Strip up to settlement, the lawless element would be forced to move on elsewhere and become somebody else's problem. Unfortunately, that hadn't happened. As a consequence, Nix presently saw the fledgling Oklahoma Territory as a vast wilderness of nothing-much. But it had enormous potential . . . potential that could only start to be realized once law and order were finally established.

And so that had become Nix's goal — to clean up Oklahoma, and clean it up for good.

At last one of the men seated across from him answered his question.

'Doolin,' said Bill Tilghman.

Nix nodded. He was fastidiously dressed in a dark wool suit and a contrasting burgundy cravat: Tilghman thought that he'd never seen a less likely-looking U.S. Marshal in his life.

'Precisely,' said Nix. 'That man has been a thorn in our side for too long, gentlemen. We need to make an example of him, if we're to stand any chance at all of winning our war on the lawless. Take out Doolin and the rest of his brethren will fall like a house of cards! And to that end, I have decided to organize a group of one hundred deputies whose sole purpose it will be to hunt this man down. You three will be the vanguard of that group. You're the best I have, and I want you to spare no effort in running Doolin to ground.'

In his assessment of the men he had summoned to his office, Nix was absolutely correct. Collectively, Bill Tilghman, Heck Thomas and Chris Madsen had been responsible for more arrests than the rest of Nix's deputies put together. They were known as his 'Three Guardsmen' and their names had slowly but surely come to be recognized and feared throughout the territory.

This close to forty, of course, Tilghman told himself he was too damn' old to be chasing across Oklahoma Territory after the likes of Bill Doolin and his Okla-hombres. Sometimes it seemed to him that the days were getting hotter, the nights colder, the trails a whole lot harder to keep travelling. And yet William Matthew Tilghman Jr. was, above everything else, a born lawman.

Before becoming a hunter of men he'd been a hunter of bison, and he'd done well enough at the trade to be able to buy a Dodge City saloon with his earnings. But Mrs. Tilghman's boy hadn't been cut out for the life of a saloonkeeper. As much as anything else, he himself was teetotal.

The upholding of the law was more to his taste, and it was something to which he'd aspired ever since he'd first clapped eyes on Wild Bill Hickok back when he was no more than fourteen years old. Even when he'd caught land rush fever and moved to Guthrie in 1889, he'd still been unable to resist the lure of the badge, and within two years he was serving as a deputy U.S. Marshal, this time working out of Chandler, OT.

Seated beside him, forty-two year-old Chris Madsen had been a soldier in the Danish Army before starting a new life here in the States. Big and bullish, with a smooth, ruddy complexion and thinning auburn hair, he had later joined the U.S. Cavalry and seen action in just about every major campaign waged against the Indians. Eventually he'd mustered out and settled on a parcel of land just west of Oklahoma City. But he'd known there could be no real setting down of roots until something was done about the territory's reputation as an outlaw kingdom. With that in mind, Madsen had become a deputy marshal, and proved to be so good at it that the newspapers had hailed him as 'a fighter who never showed the white feather.' It was an assessment Nix was happy to endorse.

Now the third Guardsman broke his long silence. 'That's easy to say, Marshal,' said Heck Thomas, swiping a finger along his fine blond mustache. 'But out there, in the territory, it's different. They like Doolin out there, they see him as a Robin Hood, who robs from the rich and gives to the poor.'

'But he does no such thing,' argued Nix.

'I have to dispute that, Marshal. From time to time he's been known to give money and food to most of the poor folks out there. Having said that, it's no surprise they like him.'

'Then I want you to make them *stop* liking him,' Nix said softly.

Madsen frowned. 'How?'

'Start spreading stories,' said the marshal. 'Tell the people he kicks dogs, rapes widows and shoots orphans. Change the public perception of him, bring the people over to *our* side. Sooner or later, one of them will spot him, and let us know where to find him.'

'That's a dirty way to wage a war,' said Madsen, his voice still heavy with his Dutch accent. 'Smearin' a man's name.'

'Well, that's the way it's going to be.'

'It's going to be hard,' rumbled Tilghman. 'After what happened at Ingalls, the people in those parts got no time for the authorities.'

'That is regrettable,' said Nix. 'But it

may surprise you gentlemen to know that I have little sympathy for the people of Ingalls. As we all know, many of them catered to Doolin's trade. They carried news of our movements to Doolin and his confederates, they furnished them with ammunition, they cared for their horses, permitted him and his men to eat at their tables and sleep in their beds. Whatever the 'good' citizens of Ingalls got, they deserved.'

'And Arkansas Tom Jones?' asked Thomas. 'Did he deserve what *he* got?'

'What do you mean by that?'

'I mean that he's small-time, Marshal, always was. It's my understanding that he only just joined the Oklahombres and hadn't yet taken part in a single crime they committed . . . and yet the courts still sentenced him to fifty years.'

'Do you consider that to be un*just*, Deputy Thomas?'

'I do, Marshal. Better to have hung him than that.'

'Then you're missing the point,' said Nix, and there was no hint of his affable smile now. 'The reason Tom Jones, or Roy Daugherty, or whatever he chooses to call himself, was sentenced to fifty years *was to set an example to others*. You're familiar with that old saw about crime not paying, I suppose?'

'Yes sir, I am.'

'Well, I am going to drive that point home to every man, woman and child in this territory, and I am going to use Bill Doolin and the rest of his gang to do so. Doolin is your absolute priority, gentlemen. And if you can't find Doolin, then you will do the next best thing, and isolate him. You will make it your business to track down every man-jack who has ever called himself an Oklahombre and capture or kill him. You will hound Doolin without mercy and turn him into a hunted man. Because a hunted man can become a careless one, and a careless one can make mistakes.'

'Or he can become a whole lot more dangerous than he is right now,' muttered Tilghman.

Nix looked at him flatly. 'Gentlemen,' he said. 'You have your orders, and they are not open to debate. I expect you to carry them out to the best of your abilities — and I expect you to begin them right *now*.'

14

Edith was now eight months' pregnant, and winter had claimed the land. As Doc Selph escorted her out to the buckboard in which she'd arrived at his office, he eyed her with clear concern.

'Sure you won't change your mind and stay here, where I can look after you?' he asked.

Muffled against the icy wind and the threat of snow that even now seemed to bruise the scurrying clouds above, Edith shook her head. 'I'm sure. Besides, I don't see as I've got much choice. Bill says it's not safe for him to come here anymore, and he wants to be with me when I have the baby.'

'I can understand that,' said Doc. 'But . . . well, he should also understand that it isn't safe for you to be traveling — not with the baby so close.'

Edith's expression told him she was

already well aware of that. 'I'll be all right. Chandler's not far, and Bill will be with me most of the way.'

'Well, if you *must* go . . . '

She smiled at him, and the smile was curiously mature for one so young. But then Doc reminded himself that she'd had to grow up fast. Anyone who spent any length of time around Bill Doolin *had* to.

Then she was squeezing one of his hands between both of hers.

'Goodbye, Doc,' she said, her eyes watering with the cold. 'And thanks for everything.'

She flicked the reins and the buckboard pulled away. Doc watched her drive off into the gloomy afternoon, and wondered what would become of her.

★   ★   ★

It was snowing steadily by the time Edith reached the large, leafless cedar tree at which she'd arranged to meet Bill, but Bill was nowhere to be seen.

She brought the buckboard to a halt and looked around her. The plain was desolate, the dirty olive-green of its tufty short grass already filling in with snow. But she consoled herself with the knowledge that Bill would be here soon. That was all that mattered.

Just then the baby kicked again.

She shook her head. How could she have considered herself to be all alone out here with Bill Junior right here inside her?

Ten minutes passed. She grew colder and colder. She was shivering hard and her teeth were chattering when a figure finally came out of the falling snow to the east, astride a gray horse she recognized immediately as Possum.

A few moments later Bill was dismounting, tying up to the rear of the wagon, then climbing as quickly as his injured foot would allow onto the seat to take her in his arms. Much as she didn't want to, she sobbed. 'Oh Bill — '

He scowled at her. 'Hey, now . . . Did you think I'd forgotten?'

'Of course not. But . . . you were so long, and — '

'I'm sorry, honey. But there's lawmen everywhere, an' not too many of the old hideouts are safe anymore.' He held her tight as the snow continued to fall around them with a feather-light pitter-patter. 'Times is changin', Edith,' he continued quietly. 'Gettin' so a man don't know who his real friends are, anymore.'

She looked up at him, sharing his concern, the concern that their way of life was changing, and there was nothing they could do to stop it.

Bill took the reins and clucked the team to a walk. The wagon shushed and crunched through the falling snow. Sometime around dusk the lights of Chandler showed in the distance.

Bill reined in on the outskirts of the small town, then climbed down and untied Possum from the rear. 'The roomin' house is at the far end of the main street,' he said, his eyelids flickering as the snow beat down on him. 'Go straight there, and I'll be along later.'

'W-When?' asked Edith, shivering.

'Soon as I figure it's safe,' he replied. 'Now — go along, woman.'

He slapped the nearest horse on the rump, stepped back and watched the buckboard roll away from him.

When it had vanished into the snow, he sagged. Ever since Ingalls, he'd had a bad feeling he hadn't been able to shake. The Oklahombres had split up for a while, maybe for good — he hadn't made his mind up about that, yet. Dick Clifton had gone into hiding until his neck wound could heal; Dalton had said something about going his own way and organizing a new gang of his own.

And then there was the exhaustion. Bill felt just about as tired as he'd ever felt in his life, and there didn't seem to be anything he could do to relieve it. He'd been living on poor food and no rest for too long now. The territory seemed to be awash with marshals, and there was never any chance to settle safely in any one place for long.

Abruptly he winced. The pain in his injured foot seemed to be getting worse, too. Some nights it nagged him so hard that he could have wept with it.

Hard as it was to do so, however, he forced himself to remain optimistic. Maybe here in Chandler he and Edith could keep their heads down and await the birth of the baby without fear of discovery. And then, once the baby was able to travel, they could leave the territory for good.

Maybe he really *could* quit the outlaw life this time, and mean it.

Maybe.

★ ★ ★

Following Bill's directions, Edith kept the wagon slipping and sliding along the deserted main street. The wind blew regularly-spaced hanging lanterns this way and that, making shadows shift and stretch.

She was glad no one was abroad to witness her arrival. It was true, what

Bill had said. Friends were becoming ever more scarce. It would be a good friend indeed who could resist the bounty that was now on Bill's head, or the promise of reward for information leading to his whereabouts.

At last the rooming house reared up out of the snow-speckled darkness. She saw that the door was decorated with a small wreath of evergreen branches with red berries attached, and for a moment she frowned at it, wondering what it was supposed to signify.

Then she realized that it was almost Christmas.

Christmas! And she'd forgotten all about it!

She struggled down off the buckboard, stepped up to the boardwalk and let herself inside.

The boarding house was run by a middle-aged woman of massive proportions, who introduced herself as Widow Stillman. The old girl labored up the stairs ahead of her new lodger, wheezing like a bellows. She led Edith along a hallway with closed doors on either side, finally stopping in front of the end room. Here she unlocked the door and allowed Edith to enter ahead of her.

Once the lamp was going, Edith saw that the room was small and sparsely furnished. But what really caught her attention was a tiny, hand-painted cardboard Christmas tree that stood atop a neat little chest-of-drawers.

Seeing Edith staring at the tree, the widow said: 'I suppose you think it's odd — me, a widow without children — bein' so fond of Christmas an' all?'

'Not really,' said Edith.

'Well, maybe it is,' the widow continued as if not hearing her. 'But — well, a body's gotta have somethin' to believe in — t' look forward to — otherwise, there'd be no reason for livin'. Right, dearie?'

Recognizing her own life in the statement, Edith nodded. 'I don't think it's odd at all.'

For an awkward beat the two women

just stood looking at each other. Around them the wind made the hotel creak. Then the widow cleared her throat and said: 'Well, let me go arrange to have your horses stabled. If there's anythin' you or your husband need, jus' you let me know. Uh . . . where *is* your man, anyway?'

'He'll be along directly.'

Widow Stillman studied her for a moment longer, then lumbered out of the room. 'Goodnight,' she called.

'Goodnight.'

When she was alone, Edith finally tore her gaze from the little Christmas tree and, unbuttoning her coat, looked down at her swollen belly. *Next Christmas*, she thought, *we'll have a tree all of our own . . . just you see.*

She was still thinking about next year, and the way things would be so different and so much better because of it, when she heard the crash of gunfire over the howl of the wind.

★   ★   ★

She spent valuable seconds telling herself that it couldn't have been what it sounded like, and even if it was, it didn't necessarily follow that it had anything to do with Bill —

Then she was at the window, struggling to lift it. The frame was stuck with paint, and fought her every attempt to move it. But even through the tarpaper windows she could hear raised voices carrying on the wind.

'It was Doolin, all right!'

No . . .

'How in hell did you recognize him? All *I* saw was a man on a horse!'

'It was the *horse* I recognized! They say he loves that damn' critter!'

The room tilted, and Edith came close to passing out but somehow clung to the window sill, still straining her eyes and ears.

A crowd was gathering in the street below now, drawn by the gunfire.

'Did you hit him?' someone called.

'I reckon!'

'Bad?'

'Dunno. Hard t' tell in all this goddamn snow!'

She stumbled away from the window then, backed toward the bed and flopped lifelessly onto its edge, trembling. Her first thought was for Bill, out there in the sub-zero darkness, possibly wounded and doubtless thinking about her. But there was something else in her now, something that hadn't been there in the beginning: a sense of weariness, a bone-deep exhaustion she had no idea Bill shared.

She was tired of living this way.

She squared her shoulders, fighting the urge to cry. Tears would do no good now, not for Bill nor for herself. She went back to the window, ungainly in her pregnancy, and looked out into the inhospitable darkness. Bill might have been spotted and recognized, but as far as she knew, he was still alive.

It was going to be rough for him in such conditions, but those same conditions would work *for* him, as well, for few locals would brave this blizzard, and the possibility that a desperate, possibly wounded man might shoot back at them if they got too close.

Bill had survived such circumstances in the past. There was no reason to believe he wouldn't survive them again. But what about next time, she thought, *next* time . . .

She couldn't go on living this way, and neither could Bill. It was no life for either of them . . . and certainly no life into which they could bring their baby.

But knowing that did nothing to lessen her fears for Bill.

Bill, out there now, in the cold, the dark, not so much a man any more as a hunted animal.

15

Edith didn't see Bill for a long time after that night, but somehow he got word to her that he was okay. He'd stopped a bullet in his left arm, he said, but told her that he'd had it doctored and since he was a fast healer, he was already as good as new. She didn't entirely believe that, and knew he was only saying it to allay her fears, but when he confessed that it had broken his heart to finally part with Possum, she saw the truth in the statement at once. Even though it made sense to do so, since it was the horse and his ownership of it that had led to the trouble in Chandler, it must have been a hard parting of the ways for him.

With the New Year Edith returned to Ingalls, once again taking her old room at Mary Pierce's hotel. Somehow she and Bill worked out a system whereby each could leave or collect messages in a wooded area just outside town. Aware that Edith might well be under surveillance, it was Mary Pierce who acted as their go-between.

On the tenth day of January, 1894, Bill collected a brief note that read: IT IS A BOY 'JAY' BORN JANUARY 9. LOVE, E.

Bill, now heavily-bearded and pared down to little more than skin and bone by life on the run, swallowed hard. A son. A *son!* But almost at once elation was replaced by despair. A son, sure . . . but a son it would be Lord alone knew how long before he could see and hold.

He had to do something or go crazy, and when he reunited with the rest of the Oklahombres at Rock Fort, he discovered that they all felt pretty much the same way.

One bitter evening they were huddled together in the dugout, discussing possible banks to hit, when there came a thumping at the door.

Abruptly silence fell across the airless little room.

The Dunns always used a special knock in order to gain entrance. The knock they'd all just heard wasn't it.

So who was outside?

Apprehensively Bee Dunn climbed to his feet and hissed: 'Douse those lamps!'

With the room lit only by the coals in the fireplace down at the far end, he went to the door and unbolted it, then climbed the steps to the second door just as someone on the other side thumped at it again. Licking his lips, Bee opened the door. A blizzard was raging outside and the wind almost tore the door from his grasp.

A man in a long, snow-encrusted Inverness overcoat was standing before the doorway, his wide-brimmed black hat tied firmly to his head with a scarf. A few yards behind him, his horse stood with its rump pointed into the storm beside that of a second man, who had remained mounted.

Bee felt his bowels loosen a little, for both men wore the distinctive six-pointed brass stars of deputy U.S. marshals.

'Saw smoke comin' from this here snowbank,' said the man in the doorway, raising his voice to be heard above the wind. 'Else we'd never've known there was a place here at all.'

Bee stared at him, recognizing him immediately even in such poor light. Not trusting himself to say anything, he remained silent.

'Blowin' a gale out here, as you can see,' the tall marshal continued. 'That's why my partner and me are looking for some shelter.'

'There's no shelter here,' Bee replied quickly.

'Not even for two men caught out in such a squall?'

'No, sir.'

The tall lawman drew a breath. 'All right,' he said, clearly trying to check his temper. 'Where in hell are we, anyway? We're lookin' for the Dunn ranch.'

'Never heard of the place,' said Bee.

'I was told it was around here someplace.'

'Well, I . . . I suggest you've done got yourself lost in this here storm,' he said. And then: 'You better go. I got no spare room for you here, an' keepin' this here door open's lettin' out such heat as I've got.'

The lawman backed away. 'No room, an' no Christian charity, looks like,' he grouched.

He stared at Bee for a moment longer, then turned and trudged back through the snow to his horse. Bee closed and bolted the door, waited until he heard the two lawman walk their horses off into the storm, then went back downstairs on legs that were weak from fear.

When he pushed back into the dugout and Tulsa Jack turned the lamps up again, he saw to his surprise that Red Buck Weightman was standing in the center of the room with his right hand curled around the grips of his Colt. Bill was standing behind him, his

172

own gun out and pressed into the small of Red Buck's back.

Pale-faced and shivering from the cold, Bee said: 'Jesus wept! Did you hear who that was? It was Bill Tilghman!'

Bill nodded. 'Ayuh. An' Red Buck here was all for puttin' a bullet in him while he had the chance.'

Bee looked from one man to the other. 'That might not've been such a bad idea,' he breathed. 'Looks like he's onto you, Bill!'

'No. If Tilghman'd thought I was down here, there's nothin' you could'a done to've stopped him comin' right in to brace me. But don't fret it, Bee. We'll be leavin' at first light.'

'You *will?*'

Bill nodded. 'I've made up my mind — we're gonna hit the Farmers an' Citizens Bank over to Pawnee. All except Red Buck, here.'

As he spoke, he stepped back and leathered his gun. At once Red Buck wheeled around and demanded: 'What was that?'

'You're through with this outfit, Weightman,' said Bill. 'We're none of us angels, but we're none of us back-shooters, either. If we have to kill a man at all, we'll kill him in a stand-up fight, not from ambush.'

'Now see here — ' began Dalton, pushing up off the bunk he'd been sitting on.

'You don't like it,' said Bill, 'you can ride out with him in the mornin'.'

'The hell with that!' hissed Red Buck. 'I'll settle this thing with you tonight!'

'I don't think so,' said Tulsa Jack.

No one had seen him draw his gun.

Weightman glared at him. After a moment he asked softly: 'That how the rest o' you boys see it?'

Bitter Creek nodded. Dynamite Dick said: 'Uh-huh.'

Weightman looked at the other men in the room, Bill Raidler and Little Dick West. 'You too?'

'As Bill says, I reckon,' said Little Dick.

Weightman shook his head like he just couldn't believe it. 'I'd've done you a *favor*, killin' that sanctimonious badge-packer!' he told Bill.

'You'd have killed one marshal,' Bill replied, 'and brought down a hundred more, all determined to find the man who shot him. We've got grief enough as it is, without addin' to it. Now, you get your head down tonight, Buck, but you be gone before dawn tomorrow. Dalton, what you do makes no never-mind to me. Me an' these other fellers, we got a bank to rob.'

* * *

The Oklahombres hit the bank in Pawnee on January 29. For Bill, it was the start of a campaign in which he hoped to amass enough money to finally quit the outlaw trail and set up a better life elsewhere with Edith and Jay.

In Woodward, on March 13, the gang stole an army payroll bound for Fort Supply. Two months later they relieved the bank in Southwest City, Missouri, of about four thousand dollars — but getting the money out of town proved to be harder than expected.

Even as they were about to make its escape, the locals organized themselves into some kind of vigilance committee. In the shootout that followed, three of the gang's horses were killed and they had to hunt up replacements under fire. Everyone caught lead to one extent or another, though none fatally. Bill himself sustained a buckshot injury just above one eye. Then Bill Raidler fired a bullet that, incredibly, passed right through one man (who survived) and killed his brother, who was standing directly behind him.

At last the Oklahombres made good their escape with a hastily-convened posse hard on their heels. After a few miles the posse lost their tracks, but the matter didn't end there. The man Bill Raidler had killed turned out to be J. C. Seaborn, a former sheriff and state senator. As a consequence, the Missouri

State Senate passed a motion to hire Heck Thomas to apprehend, capture and convict every member of the gang.

By that time, of course, Bill Dalton had left the Oklahombres. In April he and Bitter Creek tried to rob a store in Sacred Heart, on the edge of the Seminole Nation. But the store was owned by a part-time marshal named Carr, and Carr fought back. Bitter Creek took a bullet in the shoulder; Carr himself was shot dead in return.

One way or another it became clearer with every passing day that their way of life was dying. So one balmy June evening, Bill made an announcement about which he'd thought long and hard.

'It's the end of the line, boys,' he said. 'We've had a good run, more of a run than any of us could have expected when we started out together. But it's over.'

There was silence for a moment. Then Dick said: *'What?'*

'It's over, boys,' Bill repeated, the

words giving him no pleasure. 'Let's face it. We're too big and we're too famous. E. D. Nix has made it his business to take us down, and he won't stop at much to get 'er done. The rewards out on each of us'd tempt even our best friends to turn us in, I reckon.'

'That's fool talk!' growled Tulsa Jack.

'Is it? I hear the likes of Tilghman and the others've already been puttin' pressure on the Dunns. Say they know the Dunns've sheltered us before now, an' can easy arrest 'em for helpin' us, but that they'll forget about all that if the Dunns hand us over.'

'That's a lie!'

'Wish it was,' said Bill. 'But it's God's truth. Bill Dunn's already signed up as a special deputy.'

Silence but for the crackling of the small central fire filled the cave.

'Best we split up, each man goes his separate way, an' we all live to a ripe old age,' Bill finished softly.

'What if we don't want that?' countered Dick West.

'I never yet met a man who didn't want to die peaceable, in bed.'

'I met one, once,' said Tulsa Jack. 'His name was Doolin.'

'Well, that Doolin grew out of such foolishness.'

'So because of that, *we've* got to split up?'

'You fellers can do as you please,' Bill replied. 'But me, I've thought about this hard enough to make my ears bleed, and there ain't but one way to avoid the fate we all got comin' if we stick to the trail we're on. Ride on, change your name, grow a beard or shave it off if you've already got one: go north, south, east or west . . . and start over.'

'That what *you* plan to do?' asked Little Bill Raidler.

'If it ain't already too late for me, yeah.'

'Well, I never pegged you for a quitter, Bill.'

To his surprise, Bill only smiled sadly. 'Time was, I'd have whupped your butt for sayin' a thing like that.

Now I know better. I know that a man can only ride his luck so far. He gets greedy and tries to ride it any further, he generally runs it into the ground and then he's left a-foot. Don't figure to end up that way, myself.'

The announcement made, he left the cave so that they could discuss it among themselves. He wanted to feel relief, that he'd finally done what he'd wanted to do for so long. Instead he just felt lousy. He felt as if he'd let the Oklahombres down. He'd led them for as long as he'd felt like it, and now that he'd finally seen the error of his ways, he figured to desert them. He knew that wasn't so, but he knew also that was how they'd see it.

He told himself he owed these men nothing, and they owed him as much in return. But telling himself was one thing; accepting it was something else again.

16

It was full dark when Bill tied his horse in among some trees just outside of Ingalls and entered Main Street afoot. It was well past midnight, and the street was deserted. He reached the hotel, let himself inside and climbed the stairs to Edith's room. Gun in hand, he tried the doorknob. It turned silently and he let himself inside.

He paused with his back to the closed door and allowed his eyes to adjust to the darkness. Starlight showed him a shape in the double bed. He heard a soft gurgling sound coming from the crib beside it, and his throat drew tight and he wanted to smile and cry all at once. At last he shoved the gun away and crossed to the bed, cursing the rheumatism that now made his every step little short of agony.

Gently he set his weight down on the

edge of the bed, and Edith, who herself had learned to sleep light over the past several months, suddenly twitched awake. Bill reached out, put a callused palm over her mouth to stifle any cry she might make and whispered: 'It's me.'

She stared up at him, absolutely still now. Above the line of his hand, her large eyes glistened. Then he released her, she sat up and he took her in his arms and they kissed.

After a while they held each other, and Bill felt her crying softly against him, and felt full of emotion himself. Reluctantly he let her go, leaned over the crib and looked down at young Jay. The baby, his hair dark just like his father's, was fast asleep, his tiny fingers clenching and unclenching as he dreamed.

He swallowed audibly, then whispered: 'How is he?'

'Fine,' she replied. ''Course, he misses you lots, and . . . oh, Bill, you shouldn't have come!'

'Hush now, woman. I'm here now an' that's an end to it.' He stared down at the boy, entranced. 'He sure is big an' fine-lookin'.'

'But what if someone saw you? Recognized you?'

'They didn't. I made sure of that.'

He looked back at her for a long moment. Even though the gloom he could see that this life with him that was hardly any kind of life at all had aged her. The girl she'd been on their wedding day was gone, and in her place was a thin woman who looked just about as used-up as he was.

Finally he said: 'I've reached a decision, Edith. I'm givin' myself up.'

'You *what?*'

'Don't look like that. It's the only sensible thing left to do.'

'B-But they'll *hang* you!'

He'd already considered that, of course, but didn't want her to believe it could actually happen. 'Why would they do a thing like that?' he asked. 'I never killed nobody.'

'That's not what the law'll say! No, Bill,' she said, an edge to her voice now. 'No, you can't do it! I won't let you!'

'Sure you will, honey. Hell, the only reason I'm doin' it at *all* is for you — you'n little Jay, there. An' I got it all figured out. Tomorrow, I'm gonna ride over an' see Oscar Halsell. You know Oscar, he'll speak up for me. 'Sides which, he's a man of means, an' his word carries clout. I figure to ask him to go talk to Marshal Nix and ask for a pardon.'

She almost snorted. 'And you think that's what they'll give you?'

'Only one way to find out.'

She looked away from him briefly, considering his plan, the implications if it all went wrong. Finally she said: 'Well, it's a chance, I guess, even if it's only a slim one. And better to throw yourself on the mercy of the courts than to end up like Bill Dalton.'

A tingle washed across Bill's skin and he stiffened suddenly. 'What does that mean?'

She looked directly at him now. 'Haven't you heard?'

'I been too busy jumpin' at shadows to've heard much of anythin',' he replied. 'What happened to Dalton?'

'He's dead,' she said.

He went numb, whispered: '*What?*'

Briefly she told him what she'd read in the newspaper. On May 23, Bill Dalton's gang — now comprising Dalton, Jim Wallace, Big Asa Knight, Jim Knight and George Bennett — had entered Longview, Texas, there to rob the First National Bank. Bennett had been killed in the getaway, as was one bystander. Three others were wounded. About two weeks later, deputy marshals had surrounded Dalton's hideout up in the Arbuckle Mountains, and shot him dead when he leapt through a window and tried to escape.

Bill made no immediate reply. He couldn't; the news was that shocking. He'd had no great love for Dalton and wasn't about to feel sorry for him now. But that could just as easily have been him they'd written about in the paper — Bill *Doolin's* death.

He muttered something that she didn't quite catch, and she said: 'What was that, Bill?'

Without taking his eyes off the baby he repeated in a hushed tone: 'Sooner I get Oscar to speak up for me, the better.'

★ ★ ★

Marshal Nix was polite enough to hear Oscar Halsell out, but when the rancher had finished speaking, he said: 'I'm sorry, Oscar, but that's not the way we intend to deal with Doolin.'

Square-faced, with thick, center-parted hair and a walrus mustache, Halsell sat forward in the visitor's chair. He was in his late thirties but looked older, a sturdy, stocky, determined man who'd once carved an empire out of the Unassigned Lands and, more impressively, had been tough enough to hold it until country was opened up for settlement.

'What does that mean?' he demanded.

'It means that this office doesn't make deals with murderers.'

'Bill's no murderer! Why, he never killed anybody in his whole life — not even in self defense!'

'Tell that to the men who died at Ingalls. Better yet, tell it to their *widows.*'

'Bill never gunned any of those men, an' you know it!'

'Maybe not. But he's responsible, just the same.'

Halsell scowled. 'How'd you come by that?'

'The same way I'd hold you responsible if some of your boys came into Guthrie and shot the place up.'

'Oh, come *on*, now.' Halsell studied the other man for a moment, then said: 'Let's not waste each other's time any longer, Ev. We're both busy men, so let's just get down to cases. Everyone knows how much money you've poured into this manhunt of yours, how many men you've put in the field to try and catch Bill. And everyone knows you've failed time and time again! If Bill gives himself up now — even if it goes against him and the courts prove to be as intractable as you yourself — it will still count as a victory for Bill and a defeat for you.'

'That's ridiculous.'

'That's the way it is,' said Halsell with absolute certainty. 'The only way you can save face now, and justify all the resources you've plowed into this business, is to bring Bill in as a prisoner . . . or dead across his saddle! And that's *wrong*, Ev! Hell's fire, man, it's not even justice!'

'Justice is for honest men, Oscar, not the likes of Bill Doolin.'

'But . . . don't you *see?* You could end all this, right here, right now. No more expenditure, no more manhunt, no more shooting. You could end it by allowing Bill to give himself up, and you could still grab some glory from it. And yet you choose not to.'

'The law's the law.'

'Don't tell me you can't use your discretion! Look . . . Bill's a good man at heart, one of the finest I've ever known, and he's tired of running. He's got a wife and son, and he wants to go straight and be with them. Would you deny him that?'

Nix looked at him as if he were mad. 'You make him out to be some kind of saint, Oscar. He's not. He's an outlaw, plain and simple, and men have been killed in pursuit of him — *good* ones.'

'Is that your final word on the matter?'

'It is.'

Halsell snatched up his hat and climbed to his feet. 'Then I have to tell you I expected more from you than that, Evett. I expected you to be . . . impartial. But I can see now that you've taken this business just about as personally as you can.'

'That's a lie!' said Nix.

'Interesting,' Halsell said, almost to himself. 'Your mouth says one thing — but your eyes say another.'

Halsell climbed into his buckboard and left town, apparently headed back to his ranch. He kept one eye on his back-trail until he was certain he wasn't being followed, then took a little-used route through timber until, presently, he came to an open wagon, aboard which sat Bill and Edith, with little Jay sleeping contentedly on Edith's lap.

'I can see by your face that the news ain't good,' said Bill.

Halsell grimaced. 'I'm sorry, Bill. I did my best, but they just weren't interested.'

'Well, it was worth a try, I guess.'

'So . . . what now?' asked Halsell.

Bill shrugged. 'Move on to someplace where I won't be recognized, I guess. If there *is* such a place.'

'There's got to be,' said Edith.

'Well, let's hope so, anyways. In the meantime, I was thinkin' about maybe leavin' Edith an' Jay in Lawson, while I go scout out someplace else for us.'

Halsell frowned. 'What the hell is there in Lawson?'

'Edith's father runs the post office down there,' said Bill. 'An' it upset him an' Mrs. Ellsworth somethin' fierce when me an' Edith got married the way we did. Reckon it's about time they patched things up with Edith here, otherwise young Jay won't never know his grandparents.' He glanced down for a moment. 'Been a lot of trouble on account of me, one way or another,' he added. 'Like to put things right, if I can.' Abruptly he thrust out his hand. 'Thanks, Oscar — for everythin'.'

Halsell nodded, looking every inch a sad and disappointed man. 'Good luck to you, old friend. God bless you, Edith.'

If only He would, she thought.

17

After they'd made their peace, Bill left Edith and Jay with Edith's folks and once again became a hunted animal. But there was no surprise in that. Suspecting that he would try to flee the territory now that his request for a pardon had been turned down, Marshal Nix had sent an unprecedented three hundred deputies out into the field with orders to apprehend him at almost any cost.

By the end of that year he was so desperate that he and five other men attempted to rob a store in Texana, not far from the mouth of the Canadian River. They managed to steal twenty dollars' worth of stock before they were chased off at gunpoint.

As Christmas approached, Bill teamed up with Little Dick West and the pair of them rode west for New Mexico, there to change their luck. But the self-imposed exile weighed heavily upon him. His son was almost two years old now, and Bill could measure the time he'd spent with the boy in just weeks. He longed to be with Edith, too, wanted to do something to give her the things she'd always deserved — a happy marriage, a home of her own, the kind of settled, peaceful life that was the entitlement of every woman.

As the New Year got underway, the pain in his injured foot grew worse. The cold weather played hell with it, and some winter nights he hardly slept at all for the constant weakening ache of it.

Every so often news would filter through to them, but little of it was good. On April 3 the Oklahombres — now minus their leader, but once again joined by Red Buck Weightman — had robbed a Rock Island train in Dover, OT. Failing to open the safe and get their hands on the $50,000 army payroll it contained, they robbed the passengers instead, and though they got away, they soon found themselves pursued by a posse under the leadership of Chris Madsen. Eventually a gun-battle erupted, in which Tulsa Jack was killed.

That cut Bill deep, for Tulsa Jack had always been a good, loyal man to ride with, the closest thing to a real friend any owlhoot could ever expect to have.

But it didn't end there.

In July, Bitter Creek Newcomb and Charley Pierce were shot dead while they slept in the dugout at Rock Fort. Their killers, Bill, John and Dal Dunn, took their bodies in to Guthrie the very next day and collected a five thousand dollar reward.

In his lowest moments, Bill wondered if the likes of Tulsa Jack and Bitter Creek weren't the lucky ones. They were dead now, out of it. He himself was neither dead nor alive, just . . . existing.

'I got to try again,' he said one evening as he had Dick shared a mean supper of tasteless jackrabbit stew.

'Try what?'

'Try for a pardon.'

Little Dick swallowed a piece of gristle. 'You want my advice?' he asked. 'You wait it out. Nix won't be U.S. Marshal down there forever. When they get a new man in, *that's* when you ought to try for clemency. New man'll be out to make a name for himself, win himself a few votes.'

'Then maybe I ought to forget all about it, at least for now,' Bill replied, seeing sense in the argument. 'Maybe it'd be just as well if I go back, get Edith an' Jay an' try to start over somewhere new.'

'Reckon you can outrun your past?' asked Dick.

'I don't know. But I got to try it afore Jay gets much older. An' I owe it to Edith, too. It's no life at all for her.'

Dick studied him a while longer, then finally thrust out his hand. 'I wish you luck, Bill. I really do.'

Bill left their high-country hideout early the next morning and rode east, back across that part of Oklahoma still known as No Man's Land, and into an uncertain future. If he needed any more proof that Nix was continuing to wage his war on the lawless element, he received it when he heard that Tilghman had captured Little Bill Raidler near Pawhuska in September. Little Bill was put on trial for his part in the Dover robbery and sentenced to ten years' imprisonment.

Barely a week later he heard that Chris Madsen had tracked down Red Buck Weightman and killed him in the gunfight that followed.

* * *

As far as Bill Tilghman was concerned, a man didn't just drop out of sight for good and all. Sooner or later he had to show himself again, and Bill Doolin would. He *had* to.

Marshal Nix seemed to agree, for he continued to pump ever more money and manpower into the hunt for what folks were now calling the 'King of the Outlaws.'

In January 1896 Tilghman received word that Edith had left her parents' place a few months earlier, and taken her baby son with her. As far as he was concerned, there could only be one reason for that — Doolin, wherever he was, had finally sent for her.

Wasting no time, he rode to Lawson and spoke with the postmaster, who confirmed that, as Tilghman had suspected, a letter had come in for Mrs. Doolin shortly before she left, from a town called Edison, some eighty miles west. Further questioning around town turned up a witness who remembered seeing Edith and her boy travelling north in Edith's father's buckboard.

Tilghman stopped in at Lawson's only saloon and ordered coffee. As he drank it, he thought about what he'd uncovered. If Edith had headed north, then it could only mean that she was bound for Kansas, which lay no more than twenty, thirty miles from his present position.

That same afternoon he returned to the post office and sent telegrams to every town marshal or constable along the border, asking them to be on the lookout for any newly-arrived couple answering to his descriptions of Doolin and Edith, along with a baby boy, approximately two years of age.

About a week later he received a wire from the sheriff of Cowley County, who said he thought he knew the couple Tilghman was looking for. They were Mr. and Mrs. Tom Wilson and they'd taken up residence on a patch of land near the town of Burden, where they lived in a tent.

In Burden, a ranching town which sat in the shadow of the Flint Hills, the locals were quick to tell Tilghman first-hand about the couple. 'They were poor folks,' one storekeeper told him. 'Typical played-out Oklahoma boomers. And as such by no means good for my trade. But this is nothing if not a charitable town, Deputy. Just before Christmas a number of our ladies took up a collection of money and provisions for them, and rode out there to present the family with same.'

Tilghman's mouth quirked. 'Are they still out there? Living in this here tent, I mean?'

'No, sir. They stayed about three months in all, then upped stakes and moved on. Though we didn't intend it that way, I think our little show of, ah, kindness might have shamed them.'

Or maybe Bill figured they'd started attracting too much attention to themselves, Tilghman amended grimly.

'In any case, Mrs. Wilson was not a well woman,' the storekeeper went on, 'and I believe she took her child back to stay with her parents until she recovered.'

'And the husband? Did he go with her?'

'No, sir. When she left to catch the train to Perry, she and the boy were alone.'

Tilghman thanked the storekeeper

for his time, then went to grab some lunch. While he ate, he studied a map of the region. He could find no direction that looked better than another — which meant that Bill could have gone just about anywhere.

It was just then that a shadow fell across him and he looked up. A fine-looking man of about thirty was standing beside his window table, clean-shaven and turning a muley hat in his hands. He was dressed in a smart gray suit, and he wore his neatly-barbered hair short and freshly macassared.

'Marshal Tilghman?' asked the new-comer. 'I wonder if I might have a word?'

'Sure, mister . . . ?'

'Warren Graves,' said the man, offering his hand. '*Doctor* Warren Graves. I think I might be able to help you.'

'Oh?'

'I hear you've been asking around town for a man by the name of Tom Wilson?'

Tilghman narrowed his eyes. 'What about him?'

200

'I believe I know where you can find him.'

Tilghman gestured for him to take a seat. 'Go on.'

'I treated Tom Wilson not two weeks ago,' said Graves, as he took the weight off. 'He was almost crippled with rheumatism, specifically in his left foot.'

'The foot was damaged, right?'

'Yes.'

'An accident?'

'Well, that's what Mr. Wilson told me. But . . . '

'Go on.'

'It was an old gunshot wound. I'd recognize such a distinctive scar anywhere.'

'So you treated him?'

'As best I could. In the end I suggested that he might seek relief from the pain by visiting the spa at Eureka Springs.'

Tilghman frowned. 'A *spa?*'

'It's a place where the waters have certain . . . medicinal properties.'

'And Eureka Springs has such waters?'

'Yes sir.'

'And you think that's where he went?'

'I can't say for sure, obviously, but I do know he was in great pain — so much so that I think he might have been willing to try just about anything to relieve it.'

'Whereabouts is Eureka Springs?'

'It's in Arkansas,' said Graves.

Arkansas, thought Tilghman. And he said: 'Thanks, doc. You've been a real help.'

18

On January 15, Bill set off on his regular morning visit to one of Eureka Springs' many spa bathhouses to the accompanying click-click of his cane. By now he was almost unable to walk without it, and yet he was slowly but surely starting to feel better than he had in months — no, more like *years*.

The life he'd led with Edith and Jay just outside Burden had been a simple one, all too often a *hard* one, but by and large it had been a peaceful one, too. Had it not been for Edith's illness — she'd been worn down firstly by the wagon trip north to the Kansas border, and then from having to winter in nothing more protective than a patched canvas tent — and his own increasing rheumatism, they might have stayed there forever.

But here, in Eureka Springs . . . well,

it was the closest thing to Heaven that he could imagine. While the steaming, sulfur-laced spa waters helped ease the pain in his foot, his surroundings themselves did much to improve his general sense of well-being. Set in the Ozarks, and bisected by Leatherwood Creek, Eureka Springs had the kind of charm Bill had thought only ever to see in far-off Europe.

Every day since his arrival it had become his custom to take a slow walk from his lodging house to the bathhouse and bathe his foot in its restorative waters. He had no idea what they contained, only that — so far, at least — they were doing him a power of good.

Of course, he knew he couldn't stay here forever, as appealing as the prospect might be. Eureka Springs was an expensive place to live, and his bankroll had already grown dangerously thin. But he figured as soon as he was able, he'd look for work, build a new stake and then send for his family.

The thought made him smile. *Look*

for work. How many years had it been since he'd even *thought* about doing that? Whenever he needed money he'd just taken it from someone else.

Putting it that way, he felt an unpleasant prick of shame. How could he have ever justified to himself the life he'd led? And yet, back then, the money had always been secondary to the excitement. Even now he still missed that, though as he grew older and hopefully wiser, he was optimistic that there would come a time when he would no longer crave such stimulus.

His limping steps led him onto an ornate, gently bowed bridge that spanned the chuckling waters of Leatherwood Creek. When he was halfway across he stopped, leaned on the rail and looked down into the peaceful rush of water over stone. The water held about it a faintly mineral smell, and a tang of peat that reminded him of the well water he drank when he was a kid. He'd heard stories of the trout to be fished in these waters, too, and had promised himself an afternoon's fishing before much longer.

He was finally starting to relax and let down his guard, and that too was a relief. Though still tall, he was much, much thinner than he had ever been, and gray was already starting to show at his temples and in the thick beard he'd chosen to grow. His range-garb was gone, replaced by an old black-for-church suit and a boiled shirt with a string tie at his celluloid collar. Add to that the stick upon which he now had to lean, and the transformation was complete. No one looking at 'Mr. Tom Wilson' now could ever believe he had once been known as Bill Doolin.

'Good morning, my son.'

The greeting brought him back from his reverie, and he glanced around just as a tall man in priest's black walked past him, going in the opposite direction.

'Mornin', padre,' he replied vaguely, and then continued on his way.

He went three steps before he realized he knew the priest's face

— and that the face belonged to no priest at all.

He twisted around, his right hand snaking inside his open jacket for the Colt he still carried there. But the priest had turned, too, and already had a Colt of his own drawn and aimed at him.

'Game's up, Bill,' said Tilghman.

There in the center of the bridge they stared at each other. Then Bill said: 'You got the wrong man . . . padre.'

'Oh, I don't think so,' returned Tilghman. 'I've been watching you for the past three days, Bill. You've lost so much weight you hardly look like the same man you used to be. But the eyes don't change. I'd know those anywhere. They've stared down at me from dodgers just about every place I've ever been. Reckon I know them as well as I know my own.'

'Well,' said Bill, 'I'll damned if I'd've recognized you in *that* get-up.'

'That was the idea. A mite theatrical, I'll grant you, but I figured that while you might've been on the lookout for a lawman, you sure as hell wouldn't be on the lookout for a priest.' He came closer. 'I'll take your gun now, Bill.'

'Will you, now?' asked Bill, his expression unreadable.

'Let's not have any trouble. I'd hate to have to shoot you.'

'Oh, I just *bet* you would.'

'I mean it. Figure I owe you one.'

Bill frowned. 'How so?'

'Bee Dunn told me all about that night a year ago, at his dugout. About how you stopped Red Buck Weightman from shooting me down.'

'Oh, *that*. Maybe I should've let him kill you, after all. But you know somethin', Tilghman? I'm glad I didn't. I never could abide a back-shooter.'

Even before he finished speaking, he seemed to lose himself in thought again. Was this it, then; the end? A trial, a gallows, a noose? He guessed he should feel bad about that, but instead he only felt bad for Edith and Jay, that they should have had such a disappointment for a husband and a father.

'No trouble now,' warned Tilghman.

Snapping back, Bill looked back at him. 'I don't want trouble,' he replied. 'I got no desire to end up shootin' someone in the overspill.'

With elaborate care he drew his Colt and slowly passed it over to Tilghman. Tilghman tucked it away and glanced around. So far no one had seen the confrontation.

'That's better. Now — '

Without warning, Bill brought his cane up and around and Tilghman instinctively hunched up, taking the blow that was meant for his skull on the shoulder instead. As he staggered sideways, momentarily blinded by the pain of it, Bill closed in again. Hating to do it but knowing he didn't really have much choice if he wanted to retain his freedom, he brought the cane up and once again tried to crack Tilghman's skull. Tilghman recovered himself in time and grabbed the wrist holding the cane, staying the blow. At the same time he brought his Colt around and clipped

Bill on the jaw with the butt. Bill's beard absorbed most of it, but still it sent him to his knees with his head reeling.

Tilghman loomed over him, the Colt in his fist now fully-cocked.

'That was damn' sneaky,' he breathed.

'No . . . sneakier'n . . . dressin' up as a priest,' Bill returned.

'All right, we'll call it even,' said Tilghman. 'But that was it, Bill — the only chance I'm going to give you. Up, now, and let's have no more such foolishness.'

Bill pushed back to his feet, smiled bitterly, then squared his shoulders.

'All right,' he gasped. 'Let's go on home, Deputy Tilghman — an' see what fate's got in store for me next.'

* * *

When the train pulled in to Guthrie two days later, Tilghman was amazed to find that word had spread and just about every soul for a hundred miles around had descended on the rail depot to give him a hero's welcome. Even as the train slowed for its final approach, he looked through the window and saw men, women and children crammed five or six deep at trackside, all waving and cheering, with yet more clustered around the depot itself. Marshal Nix and a number of Tilghman's colleagues were there to meet him, there were reporters and a photographer on hand to capture the moment, and a local band down at the far end of the platform immediately struck up *Take Up Thy Cross and Walk With Me* as soon as the train shushed to a brake-screeching halt.

The tall marshal allowed himself a brief moment of pride. He hadn't realized the apprehension of Bill Doolin would be viewed in such a light. Feeling pleased with himself and trying not to let it show, he got to his feet and said gruffly to his prisoner: 'Come on, let's go.'

Bill, who'd been lost in thoughts of

Edith and Jay for most of the journey, looked up and smiled. 'Don't want to keep your public waitin', is that it?' he asked.

Tilghman shrugged uncomfortably. 'I didn't ask for any of this,' he said defensively.

Bill looked at him with amusement now clear in his blue eyes. 'Neither did I,' he said.

'What's that supposed to mean?' growled Tilghman, pausing partway through brushing down his lapels.

Meeting his gaze, Bill said: 'Listen. What's that them folks out there is chantin'?'

Tilghman turned and once again peered through the window. Only now did he realize that the crowd had struck up the same rhythmic chant — only now did he catch exactly what it was they were yelling.

'Doolin! Doolin! Doolin!'

'I'll be damned,' he whispered.

19

At his hearing, Bill pleaded not guilty to the charges leveled against him, and was sent to prison to await trial by jury. 'Prison' turned out to be the Federal Jail, known by its occupants as the 'Black Jail.' Situated on the north side of Guthrie's downtown district, it sat on the corner of Warner Avenue and Second Street, a blocky, red-brick building two stories high, with a flat roof and walls that were said to be nineteen inches thick.

Bill had believed he could take jail-time in his stride. Maybe he could have, if there hadn't been so damn' much of it. But what he hadn't counted on was the time the case would take to come to court.

He'd always known the wheels of justice dragged, of course, but he'd never realized just how slowly they could turn if it suited them. And keeping him in prison for month after month, making this period as much of a sentence for him as he was likely to get after the trial, gradually frayed his nerves. Whatever benefits he'd accrued at Eureka Springs soon became history.

About a week after his arraignment, he received a visit from Edith, Jay and Edith's father, Reverend J. W. Ellsworth. They sat across from each other at a bare, square table, Edith's father — a big, heavy-set man with a white mustache and cold blue eyes — making no secret of just how uncomfortable he felt to be in such a den of iniquity. Not that Bill noticed. Right then he only had eyes for Edith and Jay.

And yet to see Edith as she was now came close to breaking his heart. She looked frailer, older and sadder than he remembered, than he ever *could* remember, and he knew without any doubt that he and he alone had done this to her. As she looked back at him, her eyes filled with tears and her lips twitched and trembled.

Feeling helpless, he said stupidly: 'Don't take on, honey. Everythin'll be all right.' Impulsively he reached across the table and covered one of her hands with one of his. The other he reached out to Jay, who, seated on Edith's lap, just eyed him warily, as if he were a stranger.

And who could blame him? All the boy knew was a man who came into his life one minute and then vanished from it the next. The poor kid probably found it impossible to think of him as his father — he'd never known what a real father was like.

'Bill . . . '

He turned his attention back to Edith.

'H-how are they treating you, Bill?'

'All right,' he replied with forced good cheer. 'Food's okay. The other prisoners leave me be, me bein' such a famous badman an' all.'

'Have you seen a lawyer yet?'

'Uh-huh. Court appointed one for me.'

'And what does he think?'

'He thinks I got a good case,' Bill

replied. 'Never hurt no one I didn't have to hurt. Never killed a soul. He says if I show enough remorse, I might even walk free.'

The truth, however, was very different. His lawyer had been anything *but* optimistic about his chances. The court wanted to make an example of him, and that's what they were going to do, no matter how much remorse he showed. Still, there was no reason Edith had to know that — not yet, at least.

He looked at Edith's father. 'Look after her for me while I'm away, Reverend.'

Ellsworth grimaced. 'Her mother and I have been doing that ever since you married her!'

Edith stiffened. 'Father — '

Ignoring her, Ellsworth continued: 'I'll speak honestly, William, for that's the way I was raised, and the way I always believed I had raised Edith, until she went behind our backs and married you in secret.'

Stone-faced, Bill said: 'Go on.'

'The very sight of you *sickens* me.

You're a damned hypocrite! It's not enough just to *show* remorse. You've got to *mean* it, you've got to *want* to be saved. But *you* . . . all *you* want, all you've *ever* wanted as near as I can see, is to live the way *you* see fit, and to concern yourself not one whit with the consequences.'

'Father, that — '

Without taking his eyes from those of Ellsworth, Bill raised his hand. 'No, Edith. Let him get it out of his system. He's entitled.'

Ellsworth looked right back at him and said with feeling: 'I wish with all my heart that you had never come into my daughter's life, you and your God-less ways. I wish the Lord would answer my prayers and banish you from our lives altogether, before you corrupt your son as you have corrupted your wife.'

Bill sat back. 'Finished?' he asked.

'William, I finished with *you* years ago.'

'What happened to forgiveness?' Bill asked softly.

Ellsworth snorted. 'Forgiveness? And what, pray, would *you* know of God's teachings?'

''Be kind to one another,'' Bill said softly, ''tender-hearted, forgiving one another, as God in Christ forgave you. Ephesians, 4:32.'

For just a second Ellsworth looked as if he'd been slapped. Then he blinked a few times and said: 'Say your goodbyes, Edith. The next time we see William here, he will be on trial, and *then* you will finally see justice be done.'

★   ★   ★

The bullpen was located on the ground floor. It was a white-painted room roughly a hundred feet by sixty, where prisoners were free to roam and socialize during daylight before being locked into their cells at dusk. Hating his celebrity, Bill kept to himself as much as he could, but he could never quite get Ellsworth's words out of his mind.

Then, in late June, he was reunited with Dynamite Dick.

'They arrested me for sellin' whiskey an' sentenced me to thirty days,' Dick explained one afternoon as they sat side by side in one corner of the bullpen. 'I told 'em my name was Wiley, an' they saw no reason to doubt it. But then a deputy marshal stopped by an' recognized me. Took one look at this here neck-scar I picked up in Ingalls and re-arrested me for murder.'

'Too bad,' said Bill. 'There's only one way that'll pan out, and like as not we'll hang together — if we stay here for much longer.'

Dick eyed him shrewdly. 'You plannin' to break *out?*' he whispered.

'Not me. But you see that black feller over yonder? Name's George Lane. He was like you, got hisself arrested for selling whiskey in the Osage Nation. Well, the word is that *he's* gonna break out . . . an' when he goes, I aim to go right along with him.'

'Well, you can count me in,' Dick

said without hesitation. 'What's the plan?'

'Lane's not sayin',' Bill replied. 'But you keep an eye on him, an' be ready to move when he does.'

'I will,' Dick said with a nod. 'But he better not take too long about it. I can almost feel that noose tightenin' on me right *now*.'

* * *

Eight days after Dick's arrival Lane, a big, taciturn man with a perpetual scowl, launched his bid for escape. It was just coming on dusk when he reached through the bullpen bars and tried to fill a tin can with water from the bucket that was kept for the purpose in the corridor outside. As one of the two guards who'd been keeping a wary eye on them sauntered past, Lane suddenly grabbed him, dragged him against the bars with a clang and then repeated the move twice more in quick succession until the guard fell unconscious.

Bill and Dick immediately exchanged

looks. This was what they'd been waiting for.

Another prisoner, meanwhile — his name was Killian — quickly tore the guard's gun from his belt. Before the second guard could escape and raise the alarm, Killian had the weapon cocked and aimed.

'You want to keep breathin',' he said, 'you do like I say.'

Pale faced, the second guard reluctantly came closer with his hands held high. 'D-don't kill me,' he begged softly.

Killian tore the man's weapon from its holster and tossed it over his shoulder. Having by instinct chosen the right place to stand, Bill was there to catch it easily.

'Now open this goddamn door,' growled Lane.

When the door was unlocked, Lane led them along the corridor, through another locked door and then started unlocking all the cell doors in that wing, and telling the occupants that they were getting out.

Trailing along in Lane's wake with Dick right beside him, Bill watched the black man admiringly. Lane wasn't doing this from any sense of altruism, he simply knew there was safety in numbers — that the more men who broke jail tonight, the harder it would be for the authorities to round them all up again.

Lane had already gathered a sizeable crowd around him, Bill and Dick among them, but a great many more prisoners figured it would be safer, or maybe go in their favor, if they stayed put.

Lane saw as much for himself, and knowing they couldn't tarry much longer, began to lead his fellow escapees — now numbering fourteen in total — along the corridor to the double doors that led to the street.

As they were passing the staircase that led down to the guards' quarters, a guard came up into the corridor. Before he could raise the alarm, a prisoner named Montgomery slapped him hard with a snapped-off chair leg and he went down with barely a sigh.

They closed on the exit, two heavy black doors set into a tall archway and fastened by a padlock. Behind them someone finally yelled for help — Bill realized it was the second guard, the one the other prisoners had trussed up and left in the bullpen: he must have somehow slipped the makeshift gag they'd tied around his mouth — and suddenly there was a new urgency in them.

Lane closed on the door and without breaking stride tried to shoot the lock off.

He missed.

He tried again. Missed again.

Bill shoved him aside, took aim, fired the gun he still held and —

The padlock shattered, the chain slipped loosely through its hasp, the door was theirs for the opening.

As they poured out onto the street, it was every man for himself, and they scattered in all directions. Dick and Bill crossed the street, slipped and slid down an embankment and across two sets of railway tracks. Moments later they entered a stand of trees and just kept going.

By now Bill was breathing hard and his foot was giving him hell. Still he forced himself on, trying to ignore the pain, to concentrate only on getting away from the prison, of getting *back* to his family.

Darkness started to settle over Guthrie. Blundering through the gloom, Bill was now struggling visibly to keep up with Dick. Ten minutes later he knew he couldn't take another step, and collapsed. Dick came back, knelt beside him.

'This is a hell of a time to take a rest!'

'I . . . I'm sorry . . . just . . . can't go no . . . further. This damn foot of mine — '

'Well, you sure can't stay *here,*' muttered Dick. 'They'll catch you for sure.'

'You . . . go on. I'll take my . . . chances alone.'

'Hell with that,' said Dick. 'Come

here. I'll carry your sorry hide if I have to.'

'You do that and they're catch us *both.*'

Dick grinned through the darkness. 'I'll risk it.'

Bill looked up at him then, and suddenly, unaccountably, found himself thinking of all the people he'd known and lost along the way; of Tulsa Jack and Bitter Creek, of Charley Pierce and even the likes of Bill Dalton and Red Buck Weightman; and the likes of Arkansas Tom Jones and Little Bill Raidler, now spending what years they had left behind bars.

Then:

'Listen!'

Dick's whisper brought him back to the present. Bill stared at him, hearing it as well.

Dogs.

The guards were tracking the escapees with hounds!

'Damn!'

'We gotta go, Bill!'

'Help me up.'

But it was all he could do to stand, much less walk, and certainly not run.

Then they heard a new sound, coming from someplace up ahead of them. A wagon, coming closer.

'Give me that gun,' said Dick, and when he had it in his hand he ran toward the edge of the timber, where a thin trail cut between the woods. The moment Dick saw it he also spotted the buggy traveling along it at a steady walk, a young man in a suit at the reins.

Picking his moment, Dick broke cover just as the buggy drew parallel to his position, and he quickly snatched at the horse's cheek-strap.

'Whoa, there!' he snapped, and instinctively the young man on the seat dropped the reins and raised his hands.

'What . . . what . . . ?'

'Get down off there!'

The young man looked terrified. 'I . . . I don't have any money! I'm just a schoolteacher, and — '

'We . . . only want your . . . buggy,'

gasped Bill, breaking cover to join them.

He limped around to the far side of the buggy and hauled himself aboard even as the young schoolteacher climbed down, anxious not to anger his attackers. Dick climbed up beside him, took the reins and started to turn the vehicle around.

'B-but . . . ' said the young man, 'you can't just leave me here!'

'Watch!' said Dick — and slapped the horse into a trot.

★　★　★

When they judged themselves to be safe from further immediate pursuit, Bill and Dick split up. Dick took the gun, Bill took the horse, and with a short but firm handshake, each went his own way, never to see the other again.

Bill knew the first place they'd look for him was at the Ellsworth farm, where Edith and Jay were still living. So he traveled southwest instead, until a forty-mile ride brought him back to one of his earlier hideouts down along the Cimarron. Hiding out in a cave not far from Beaver Creek, he spent the next six weeks living a pretty much hand-to-mouth existence while he tried to figure out his next and best course of action.

He was more now determined than ever to put the outlaw life behind him. Edith and Jay deserved better than he'd given them so far, and if it wasn't already too late, he intended to spend the rest of his life making it up to them.

And then, one lonely August evening he remembered that he knew a pretty good feller by the name of Rhodes, who lived in New Mexico. Rhodes was a smart feller who ranched and wrote stories for a living. More than once he'd allowed Bill to lay low on his land, and now Bill wondered if it might be possible to start a new life there, with Edith and Jay, in the so-called Land of Enchantment.

The more he thought about it, the more he liked the sound of it.

His mind made up, he finally dared to start moving around again, and calling in some old favors he was able to outfit himself with a fresh horse, new clothes, a handgun and rifle. After that he was ready to embark on a cautious ride north and east, headed for Lawson ... and what he hoped to be the turning point in his life.

20

Heck Thomas crouched in cover on a brush-littered hillside overlooking the Ellsworth house, watching as Edith and her mother packed a few meager supplies in the back of the family buckboard. Reverend Ellsworth stood in the doorway with the boy, Jay, in his big arms. He watched the women work but made no attempt to help them. Whatever was going on, he clearly disapproved of it.

At last Edith threw a tarpaulin over her few possessions and then set about tying it down.

'*Still* think he ain't gonna show up?' asked Bee Dunn, who was hunkered beside Thomas in a scattering of buck-brush. 'I mean, that woman down there, she's sure fixin' to go *somewheres* tonight.'

It was all Thomas could do not to

230

grimace at Dunn's proximity to him. About a week earlier, Dunn had come to see him in Guthrie with information he said would lead to the arrest of Bill Doolin. Remembering how they'd calm-as-you-like shot Bitter Creek Newcomb and Charley Pierce dead while they slept at Rock Fort, Thomas had little time for the Dunns, but out of courtesy asked him what it was. Dunn had replied that he wasn't about to tell anyone that until he had it in writing that he and his brothers would get their share of the sizeable reward that had now been posted on Bill's head.

That figured.

Thomas had discussed the matter with Marshal Nix, who told him they couldn't afford to ignore any information, no matter its source. So Thomas had provided Dunn with a note guaranteeing him his share of the reward money if his information panned out, after which Bee had said: 'He's on his way back to Lawson, right this minute.'

'How'd you come to know this?'

'Friends o' mine down in Payne County, they seen him. Said he was gettin' set to pull out for good. Hear tell as how he's fixin' to collect his wife an' boy and take 'em west.'

'How reliable is this information, Bee?'

Bee had cracked a lopsided grin at him. 'Trust me, Deputy, I wouldn't've come all this way if it weren't good.'

Still only half-convinced, Thomas organized a posse which included three of the Dunn brothers, Tom and Charley Noble, a big, soft-spoken black deputy by the name of Rufus Cannon and Thomas's own son, Albert. His thinking was that, if the Dunns were right, then Thomas was going to make history when he brought Doolin to book, and he wanted his eldest boy there to see it.

Now Albert broke into his thoughts with a low-voiced: 'Where you figure on layin' for him, pa?'

In the fading daylight, the boy looked younger than his years, and Thomas suddenly wondered at the wisdom of having fetched him along.

'There's no need for his woman to see us arrest him,' he replied. 'We can save them that much, I reckon. Rufe?'

Rufus Cannon said: 'They's a cane field jus' west a piece — be good cover for us, an' Doolin'll have to pass through it to get here.'

'Okay,' said Thomas. 'Then that's where we'll wait for him.'

* * *

It was the better part of a hundred and sixty miles to Lawson, and Bill made practically the entire journey under cover of darkness. Now, as he closed on the Ellsworth place, he knew better than to expect a warm welcome from Edith's father. The man had never liked him, and Bill really couldn't say that he blamed him. But whether Ellsworth would believe him or not, he intended to swear that from now on he would take care of Edith and the boy just the way he should have all along.

The wide Oklahoma sky was a

power-blue bowl, dusk was coming on fast and stars were already starting to show. He'd written to Edith a week earlier, telling her of his plans for her and Jay, and asking her to get them both ready for travel. He hadn't been specific about their eventual destination in case his letter should be intercepted, only that she'd like it, and the climate would probably help with his rheumatism.

A few yards on he drew rein and swung down from the saddle. Never mind his foot right now — his butt was aching something fierce! He stretched to ease the kinks and drew in a deep draught of good, clean summertime air. It had been a heck of a ride, but he'd made it at last.

He took out his knife, opened it up and deftly cut down a cane. Then, leading his bay mare behind him, he started limping along the trail, his thoughts dominated by images of his wife and son. He was in such high spirits now that he'd even started whistling.

*   *   *

'Edith,' said her mother, joining her in the neat little Ellsworth parlor, 'you'll wear that window out, the way you're staring through it.'

Edith turned away from the window with a faint blush. 'I'm sorry, Mother, I just can't help it. It's been so long since I saw him, and I know it's going to be different this time — '

'I hope so,' said Mrs. Ellsworth, studying her with concern. 'Because if it isn't — '

'It *will* be,' Edith insisted.

The older woman inclined her shoulders, not entirely convinced. 'Well, just so long as you know you'll always have us to come back to.'

Edith pulled a face. 'I'm not so sure about that. Father — '

'Your father has his way of looking at things,' Mrs. Ellsworth reminded her, lowering her voice because Jay was playing with his colorful building blocks just a few feet away, in front of the hearth. 'But he loves you, Edith, he worries for you and only wants you to be safe and happy.'

'I *will* be, when Bill gets here,' she said.

Her mother studied her for a long beat. 'You never stopped loving that man, did you?' she asked, almost in wonder. 'Even after all he put you through.'

'Not a-once,' Edith replied. 'But there's been plenty of times when I felt I was the only one who ever really saw the goodness in him.'

Mrs. Ellsworth's eyes suddenly filled with tears. This wasn't the way she'd wanted her daughter's life to work out, but if only she *could* find happiness in it at last, then all the misery would have been worthwhile.

Impulsively she hugged Edith to her. 'Well,' she said in a voice choked with emotion, 'he'll be here any minute now, Edith. Then all the waiting will be over.'

'Yes,' replied Edith. 'And I can hardly wait. In fact . . . ' She suddenly crossed the room and scooped up her shawl

— the same white woolen shawl in which she'd been married three years earlier.

'What are you doing?' asked her mother.

'I'm going to walk through the cane fields,' said Edith, 'and meet him.'

Jay looked up from his toys and watched her leave.

★ ★ ★

'That's far enough, Bill!'

As soon as Heck Thomas's voice rang out Bill froze in his tracks, not so much surprised, not even so much angry, as just . . . disappointed. For weeks now, he'd allowed himself to think that he might actually be able to walk — limp — away from this life after all. He'd dared to let himself relax a little, and think that just maybe he'd outsmarted the law after all, would have the last laugh on Nix and his deputies and live out the remainder of his days in blessed anonymity.

Now he suddenly knew better.

For a moment silence hung thick over the gloomy cane fields. Then came the soft, shushing sounds of men in motion and the gentle clicking of canes being pushed aside as Thomas and his men broke cover with rifles and shotguns leveled. Even though the light was fading fast, Bill recognized the Dunns and his lip curled disgustedly at the sight of them.

'This is Deputy U.S. Marshal Thomas,' called Thomas.

'I know who you are,' said Bill. He looked off toward the east and thought bitterly: *Not even half a mile to go now. Just half a mile to Edith an' Jay.*

'Then you know I'm here to take you in,' said Thomas.

'I know you're here to *try.*'

Bill let go of the reins and his mare wandered off to chew at the sparse grass alongside the trail. He thought about all the plans he'd made, about the new life he'd intended to start, and knew now that unless there was a miracle in the offing, it was never going to happen.

He *did* feel anger then.

'Don't do anything foolish, Bill,' Thomas warned. 'I'm callin' upon you to come peaceable.'

Bill didn't respond. The idea of being thrown back into the Black Jail, made to wait week after week, month after month, until his trial date was set . . . and then like as not to be sentenced to hang at the end of it just so's E. D. Nix could set his precious *example* didn't appeal to him.

But then, neither did dying . . .

It was then he remembered what Edith's father had said to him that day in Guthrie; the thing he had never been able to get out of his mind in the days that followed.

I wish with all my heart that you had never come into my daughter's life, you and your Godless ways. I wish the Lord would answer my prayers and banish you from our lives altogether, before you corrupt your son as you have corrupted your wife.

The thought suddenly made him choke up with emotion. All at once he was so tired of the life he'd made first for himself and then for Edith, the kind of life he was making even now for Jay. He was thirty-eight years old and he felt more than twice that age. He was worn out, a cripple whose injured foot was a constant reminder of the life he'd led.

I wish the Lord would answer my prayers and banish you from our lives altogether, before you corrupt your son as you have corrupted your wife.

He saw it clear as day, then; as hopeless as things looked, it was still within his power to make up for the misery he'd brought to Edith and the uncertainty he'd given to Jay. He saw a way to do something *good* for once. But it meant —

. . . before you corrupt your son as you have corrupted your wife.

'You hear me?' said Thomas. 'Put your hands up and you won't get hurt.'

Abruptly the silence around Bill grew

deafening. Then he reached his decision and called back: 'Sorry, Heck. I don't think there'll be any surrenderin' here today.'

And throwing away his cane, he went for his gun.

★ ★ ★

Hurrying through the twilight, Edith suddenly broke stride and clutched the shawl a little tighter around her. She wanted to believe the sound she'd just heard was thunder, but there wasn't a cloud in the sky.

Then if it wasn't thunder . . . ?

No . . . no . . .

Desperately wanting to believe that it was anything other than what she knew it to be, she suddenly broke into a run, screaming: 'Bill! *Bill!*'

Almost as one the posse opened fire on Bill. And for an instant he felt the blinding agony of bullet and buckshot as his chest was literally shredded.

Then the impact of all those slugs

and pellets hurled him backward and he collapsed on the dirt. He lay there for a moment, coughing blood, gasping for air, staring at the sky as it seemed to grow darker. It took great effort for him to breathe. But, strangely, he felt no pain ... felt nothing except for a growing chill.

And then, wonder of wonders, he *swore* he heard Edith calling his name. It gave him great comfort, because he could think of no better way to die than to take the sound of her sweet voice with him.

★ ★ ★

The posse approached Bill's body warily, guns still at the ready.

'Bill!'

The men all turned as Edith came rushing out of the darkness, skirts swirling around her. As she shoved through them, Thomas swore, for he hadn't meant for her to see what she was now about to see — Bill sprawled on the ground, his shirt riddled with holes, the material stuck to the feeble rise and fall of his chest with glistening blood.

She screamed at the sight — a sound Thomas knew he would never forget — and almost collapsed to her knees beside her husband.

Between sobs all she could manage was: 'Bill . . . Bill . . . '

He reached up one hand, closed his fingers weakly around her arm and looked up at her as if she were nothing more than a figment of his imagination. His face was pale, his eyes sunken, and there was bright, bubbly lung-blood at his lips.

'Edith . . . ?' he whispered.

She held his arm tighter. 'I'm h-here, Bill . . . I'm here.'

He swallowed dryly. ' . . . gave 'em what they . . . w-wanted . . . '

'Shhh, now. Don't try to speak — '

' . . . s-second chance . . . '

She nodded, fighting tears. 'Y-Yes, Bill. Th-that's right. Y-You're going to get a second ch-chance.'

Somehow he found the strength to shake his head. 'N-Not for . . . me, sweetheart. F-For you. And Jay.'

She frowned and started to say she didn't understand.

But she was too late.

Bill exhaled one final time . . . and then was gone.

*   *   *

Heck Thomas looked down at the corpse for a long, shocked moment.

'Damn,' he said.

He'd never expected it to end like this. He'd thought —

But to hell with what he'd thought. Stooping, he gently helped Edith to her feet. As she straightened up, she was unable to take her eyes off from the man she'd loved and now lost.

Thomas cleared his throat. 'I'm sorry, Mrs. Doolin,' he said sincerely. 'It's not the way I wanted this to play out. But he gave us no choice. I asked him to come along peaceable and instead he went for his gun.'

She looked at him with eyes that were glazed by shock, and said: 'You . . . you're wrong.'

''Fraid not, ma'am. That's exactly how it was.'

'I-It couldn't be,' she said, lifelessly.

'I promise you — '

'Look,' she said, and pointed.

'I'm tellin' you, ma'am — '

'*Look, damn you!*'

Thomas looked at the corpse and saw for the first time that Bill's gun was still in its holster. And as the truth of what had really happened sunk in, the lawman thought, *Oh my God*.

The outlaw who'd sworn he'd never killed a man in his life had no intention of killing anyone today, either. He'd only *pretended* to go for his gun. And there could only be one reason for that. Given no other choice in the matter, Bill had wanted things to end this way.

Edith realized the same thing in the same moment, suddenly understood

245

what Bill had been trying to tell her about giving the authorities what they wanted in order to give her and Jay a second chance.

'Bill . . . ' she whispered. 'Bill . . . '

★   ★   ★

Though it would be many months before she could finally accept what he'd done and the reasons behind it, Edith knew immediately that with this one single, selfless action, Bill Doolin had atoned for every mean thing he had ever done or had ever been accused of doing. Such was his love for her and for Jay that he'd made the ultimate sacrifice . . . and made it willingly.

He had died as he'd lived.

As a man.

As an Oklahombre.

THE END

MEAN AS HELL
DRAW DOWN THE LIGHTNING
HIT 'EM HARD!
DAY OF THE GUN